KU-184-927

COLD RELATIONS

Edinburgh's gorgeous Detective Sergeant Honey Laird had finally cleared her overflowing desk and was looking forward to spending some time with her husband when an email from her old school friend provoked yet another difficult case. Honey soon finds herself trying to babysit her friend's ex-husband Andrew: a trigger-happy, former SAS officer, with a temper, a head injury and a penchant for attractive women.

COLD RELATIONS

COLD RELATIONS

by

Gerald Hammond

Magna Large Print Books
Long Preston, North Yorkshire,
BD23 4ND, England.

British Library Cataloguing in Publication Data.

Hammond, Gerald
    Cold relations.

    A catalogue record of this book is
    available from the British Library

    ISBN   0-7505-2532-0

First published in Great Britain in 2006 by
Allison & Busby Ltd.

Copyright © 2006 by Gerald Hammond

Cover illustration © Old Tin Dog

The moral right of the author has been asserted

Published in Large Print 2006 by arrangement with
Allison & Busby Ltd.

All Rights reserved. No part of this publication may be
reproduced, stored in a retrieval system, or transmitted in any
form or by any means, electronic, mechanical, photocopying,
recording or otherwise without the prior permission of the
Copyright owner.

Magna Large Print is an imprint of Library Magna Books Ltd.

Printed and bound in Great Britain by
T.J. (International) Ltd., Cornwall, PL28 8RW

Chapter One

Ask any random group to choose the most attractive woman from another group and you will find that different choices will be made by the women as against the men. The reasons are simple. Each sex will have taken into account the usual criteria of beauty discarding those with any tendency to obesity, sagging, asymmetry or deformity. Out will have gone those with raddled skins, a serious squint or an unfriendly cast of features. The chosen ones will be smoothly rounded in face and body, with pleasant expressions. They will conform to the stereotypes of youth – round eyes, long legs, smooth skin and not too large a nose.

But the above reads like a general specification for female beauty. The difference between the gender choices is explained by the form of the question. Beauty is almost universal, subject to local or temporal changes of fashion. Attractiveness, while incorporating the same criteria, introduces others. The women judges may have made choices based only on beauty but perhaps with a slight bias towards masculinity. Men will have sought out femininity, even feminine sexual promise – an hourglass figure, rounded hips, prominent breasts, pouting lips and perhaps slightly hooded eyes.

Honoria Laird, without actually displeasing the women judges, could have been sure of the masculine vote. Of this she seemed quite unaware, although if her mirror had not given her the assurance she might have known it from the fact that for a few months after leaving finishing school, until her father put his foot very firmly down, she had modelled expensive lingerie for a living. She was tall for a woman and accorded well with the criteria already outlined. Her dark hair had a natural curl. Her full lips were well-modelled, her brown eyes large and bright and her expression in repose was a piquant mix of dignity and humour. She had a natural sense of style and could have dressed well on a comparative pittance, but a very generous allowance from her landowner-industrialist father was an undeniable help.

She had been born Honoria Potterton-Phipps. As a pretty baby and while her early hair remained fair, it was inevitable that she would be called Honeypot; and as her hair grew darker and she grew from a tomboy into a beautiful woman, even after her marriage changed part of the basis for the pun, the nickname stuck. This she found puzzling. When she grumbled to Sandy, her husband, he tried to explain that she attracted men like flies to a honeypot, but she told him to pull the other one. 'Honeypot' was not a suitable nickname for a police officer of some seniority. She liked to be called Honey, in the American manner, and was so addressed by most of her friends. The name was apt, her hair being much the colour of dark heather honey. Her subordinates, behind her back, used either nickname but the sobriquet Honeypot was only accepted, face to face, from the chosen and favourite few.

For no particular reason that she could remember she had at one time joined the Metropolitan Police, where her natural ability, remarkable memory and Criminology degree had soon raised her to Detective Sergeant. When she met Detective Inspector Alexander Laird on a firearms course the attraction was immediate. Sandy Laird was an officer with the Lothian and Borders Constabulary, based in Edinburgh. Honey had been born and largely raised on her father's estate in Perthshire so that a return to Edinburgh was almost a coming home; while Lothian and Borders were delighted to poach a Detective Sergeant, trained at Hendon, from the Met.

After a period at Newton Lauder, she was brought in to Edinburgh. It was a convenient opportunity for the couple to wed, and wed they did.

In the police, a certain amount of joking, even horseplay, is tolerated; but a woman officer with ambition must aim to retain respect. Honey cultivated an air of dignified reserve and her occasional inclination towards frivolity was restricted to her home life and to her correspondence with her many friends.

The beginning of this story was gradual. A convenient but randomly chosen starting point finds her sitting alone and busy at her laptop computer in the small office that she usually shared with three colleagues. A passing colleague, glancing in, might have supposed that the typing pool was busy and that she was writing reports or otherwise catching up with the paperwork that has been invented solely to plague the busy officer. But she was a quick and efficient typist and had the knack of composing lucid

10

English at speed. Her paperwork was finished and her casework delegated and she was busy writing an email to a friend.

She wrote:

11 December. Edinburgh.
Poppy darling, I know it's an age since I last emailed you, but I hadn't forgotten you and I promise that I would have written soon even if I hadn't had your email last week. Truly. But life has been full and busy. Did I tell you that I'd been made up to Detective Inspector? Well it's true, and it leaves me very short of people with whom I can let my hair down. Most of my days are spent pretending to be an infallible prig. An old school-friend living a long way away makes an ideal correspondent.

I may say that I was perfectly happy as a DSgt in Lothian and Borders. The extra money doesn't even make much difference – as you know, I have an extremely wealthy Dad who thinks that I'm still his little girl and also a husband who is preceding me up the promotion ladder. The downside is that I still have responsibility for the dog unit while working several cases of my own and I remain responsible to the loathsome Det Sup Blackhouse of evil memory. He started off hating my guts, but he now thinks that I'm the best thing since flavoured condoms, which is worse because he drops all the weirdest cases in my lap with an air of doing me favours.

That's enough about me. Now to the matter of your email. You told me once, in fact rather more than once, that your first husband and the father of your twins was a louse and a rat, which is pretty much how I remembered him from the few occasions on which I'd met him. Judging from your present anxious enquiries, I now suspect that you still have fond feelings for him. Well, I can understand you divorcing him, but should you really have married again so precipitately? He had only had it away with Julia Foster, and we remember what round heels she always had. Talk about burning your bridges!

Anyway, as requested I tracked your ex down today and I must say that he no longer shows any signs of being the arrogant bastard that I remember from your wedding and one or two other occasions. If that's what a head-wound does for you, we'll have to arrange for most men to be shot. (Not Sandy, of course, he's a pussycat, although he acts very tough when it seems to be called for). The head-wound seems to have had much of what I understand to be the effect of a pre-frontal lobotomy. You couldn't give me an address or even a phone number, you only managed to tell me that he had returned to the vicinity of his native Edinburgh, and there are several Andrew Grays registered with Social Services, so pinning him down took a little time.

I can now report that the post-Iraq Andrew Gray seems well and happy within his limits. He is living a monastic life, from all reports, just outside Edinburgh in the small house his aunt left him. She also left him a little money, so with that and his disability pension he seems to be getting by. He is not the sharpest stake in the fence, but then you will probably say that he never was. But does intelligence bring happiness? The reverse, I rather suppose. You have to be daft to be happy in this life. The difference in his case is that he now seems very placid and rather slow. There are signs of discontent with the life of idleness but I don't honestly think that he's fit for employment. According to his record he can flare up suddenly. He was fined quite heavily for a punchup outside a pub and only his history and decorations saved him from the jug. The other man seems to have started it by assuming that slow means soft, but the courts look askance at ex-SAS officers who engage in fisticuffs with members of the public, especially if the member ends up with a broken jaw.

He recognised me immediately, addressing me as Honeypot in front of a social worker and a constable who happened to be in the car with me at the time. (I have still not shaken off that sobriquet entirely although it is several years since I ceased to be Honoria Potterton-Phipps. Sandy says that it's only to be expected but he won't explain why.) Andrew immediately asked me to help him to regain his shotgun certificate, but with that conviction on his record I don't see a chance; and I wouldn't be happy to have somebody with a hair-trigger temper walking around armed. Frankly, I'm not too happy that he's driving, because I can well imagine an incident of road rage.

He fishes a bit, but that doesn't keep him occupied. He has been helping a local keeper and goes beating quite often, but he doesn't really feel part of the scene that he used to know and love. When I probed a bit to find out what he really missed, it turned out not to be knocking down the pheasants. He said quite solemnly that when you've shot people in the line of duty, pheasants seem a bit tame. I suppose there's a certain amount of rather wacky logic in that. It was the dog-work and the company of men who were preoccupied with dogs and wildlife that he used to find congenial. (Don't take this the wrong way, but I think that he misses your dogs more than he misses you.) He would have found it difficult to keep a dog while he was still in the army.

*I suggested that he now had the perfect oppor-
tunity to keep a dog. At the time, I was only
thinking of providing him with some company
and something to nurture. He jumped at the
idea and wanted to rush down to the dogs' home
to adopt a stray; but, however desirable it is to
get unwanted dogs rehomed, he wouldn't know
what he was getting in a rescue dog or whose
mistakes he was inheriting. (This goes double for
dogs that have failed the guide dogs course,
which was his first thought – they must be dim
or unruly and, in addition, they have been
taught to walk in front instead of at heel.) I
pointed out that he would be much better
starting with a pedigree pup of one of the gundog
breeds. Then he could go beating and picking-up
and not feel left out of it at all, and training a
pup would take up much more of his time than
accepting an adult dog that had been taught or
mistaught by somebody else. And why would the
dog be available for rehoming? Bad luck in the
family or an evil disposition?*

*Here let me point out, Poppy darling, that
Andrew Gray is your ex- and not mine. I know
you can't come rushing back from Monaco
every time your former husband gets his head in
a sling. I'll do what I can, within reason, but
Andrew is still a handsome devil, the scar seems
to add to rather than detract from his rather*

*piratical good looks, and what Sandy will say if
I see too much of him I just do not know. I'll go
this far. If you care to make a donation towards
the cost of a suitable puppy, I'll match it and see
that he doesn't get ripped off.*

*If you have an excuse to revisit Scotland, come
and stay again. Your last visit was marred by the
sudden murder case requiring every available
body, but life isn't always like that. Often but
not always. And we did have some fun before the
storm broke, didn't we?*

All the best, Yours, Honeypot.

Chapter Two

DCI Sandy Laird looked fondly at his wife and thought how lucky he had been. Not only a character who was splendid to live with – funny, sympathetic and wickedly good in the marital bed – but lovely enough to make all his colleagues jealous. What more could a man wish for? Sometimes he wished that she had not come from a family to which money was of little account; at others, he knew perfectly well that she sometimes, secretly as she thought, eased their path with a little greasing with her father's money. She was never extravagant. He pretended ignorance and thanked his lucky stars that he did not have to grudge her anything that she really wanted.

Honey usually felt just as fortunate, but surely a husband *ought* to have just a trace of jealousy. 'You really don't mind me driving around with a good-looking and unattached male?' she asked. Could it be that he didn't care? Or that he felt guilty about something and was making up for it?

Sandy became aware that he was treading on dangerous ground. They were entering territory wherein almost any answer was likely to be wrong. He gave her a hug and then nibbled her earlobe. 'I trust you absolutely,' he said. 'And, of course, you'll drive him mad with lust but I know you're capable of dealing with any would-be lover.'

'He's ex-SAS.'

'He's spent months in hospital since those days and from what I hear he's very well behaved.'

She turned her head to put the earlobe beyond his reach. 'The sheriff didn't think so. Why don't *you* go with him?'

He sighed and spoke with exaggerated patience. 'Darling, you know I'm right in the thick of it. The McLure case is taking up rather more than all my time. And these are your friends, not mine. And also, you know more about dogs than I do. If you feel the need for a chaperone, get one of your friends to go with you.'

'They'd think that I was trying to set them up on a date.'

'That might be a sound idea in itself. What he needs is a companion-nanny-mistress. What about June?'

The two were cramped together in one

overstuffed armchair. As he spoke, he felt Honey's body stiffen. June was their resident maid, daughter of Honey's father's housekeeper, a treasure and an absolute necessity while both were working and liable to be called to duty suddenly at any time. Sandy was unnecessarily touchy about being seen to accept subsidy from Honey's father, who was an industrial tycoon as well as a major landowner. He never acknowledged that his wife was underwriting part of June's wages out of her allowance from her father.

'You're not thinking that we might put her forward for the post?' Honey enquired.

'Lord, no! Life would be impossible without her. Imagine one of us away and the other coming home late to a cold and empty house. Let him find his own nursemaid. I was only suggesting her as your escort for the afternoon.'

'Keeping house for us is what she's for. I suppose I'll have to face him without backup,' she said. 'Remind me to take that can of Mace® with me. Well, at least a dog should help him to meet people. I thought a Labrador. You can't really go wrong with a Lab. Treat them well and they train themselves and they'll love you for ever after whether you deserve it or not. You can't beat a Lab.'

They were stretched out in the chair – which must have been built for somebody of enormous girth – in their sitting room, each relaxed after a good meal but tired after a hard day. She stretched out a long and well turned-leg and gave Pippa, her personal Labrador, a push. The dog responded with an affectionate fart.

'Sometimes they make you want to beat them. Nothing can eat or fart like a Labrador. They leave all other breeds at the farting gate. You think he's capable of looking after a dog properly?' Sandy asked.

'I'm sure of it. He's not an idiot. He's a bit slow and very gentle and I think he's just looking for something to lavish all his bottled-up love on. I phoned that chap in Fife, the Lab breeder, and he has a bitch puppy available. If that doesn't work out, we'll try again after Christmas when the un-wanted presents are being returned. As soon as Andrew gets a puppy of his own he'll forget all about me.'

'All right. Carry your mobile phone switched on and I'll do the same.'

Two days later, Honey emailed to her friend Poppy:

Poppy – before I forget, let me wish you a very Happy Christmas and a thoroughly happy New Year. Now to matters of more importance.

Your money order arrived safely. I said earlier that you must still have a tendresse for your ex and to judge from the size of your money order you must still be his slave. But I said that I'd match your contribution and I'm not one to renege. I wasn't sure whether it would be best to try before Christmas while pups were still available or later when unwelcome presents had been returned. I decided to start now. To my surprise Sandy was not in the least perturbed at the idea of my driving all over the place in the company of a personable ex-officer with a history of brain damage and loss of temper. I did ask Sandy whether he'd rather undertake the chore. But he said that I know more about dogs than he does and anyway he's in the thick of a big fraud case just now.

According to Dad's 'keepers the most suitable breeder, or the one with the most suitable line of Labs, was in north-east Fife, not too far away. Even if it hadn't looked like snow, I wasn't going to travel in Andrew's little sports car and come back with a wet puppy being sick in my lap. Dad, you may recall, still passes his Range Rovers on to me as soon as he gets tired of the colour or the ashtrays are full or something. We went in the latest handmedown. *Rather than have Andrew's rusty little toy lowering the tone outside our house all day, I picked him up from his door. I brought Pippa along because she's a motherly bitch who would reassure any pup on the journey.*

We had directions to a Joe Little, who breeds (and trains and competes with) the most perfect Labradors. Only when we were there did Andrew mention that what he really wanted was a springer spaniel. I didn't slap him – he might have hit me back and he's SAS trained. I did try to point out that springers, being self-willed and cussed little bastards, were a challenge for the beginner, that they collected mud and burrs like nobody's business and that after being out of doors for ten seconds in a slight drizzle you could wring them out like a sponge, but it went through and out of the other ear without touching the sides.

Well, I know what it is to have the courage of your prejudices so I ground my teeth but didn't argue. We were about to slink away when Mr Little mentioned a spaniel breeder only a few miles away who he said that he could strongly recommend. I could see that Mr Little was very well organised and he had admired Pippa, so his recommendation should count for something. He mentioned that the spaniel kennel-name was Throaks, which you see quite often figuring in the results of field trials, so we went along there.

We found Three Oaks Kennels (although the third oak is little more than a sapling, its predecessor having come down in a gale, but the other two are enormous). It is another well-run business, well kept and with lots of contented-looking spaniels of different ages. John Cunningham, who I took to be the senior partner, turned out to be another ex-officer invalided out and as soon as this fact emerged the two were off bandying reminiscences and I was left to prowl the kennels on my own. I didn't mind too much. There was a cutting wind and the first flakes of snow, but dogs are warm to handle. I always enjoy socialising with good dogs and I brought away one or two useful ideas for the dog unit. The two men were still re-fighting the Falklands and it took some strong hinting from me to reintroduce the subject of dogs.

Being a Labrador-fancier myself my mind had been running on Labs, but it turns out that springers are not quite as expensive. A trained or half-trained dog would have met the case and been within budget. But no. Nothing would do for your ex but to start with a pup, and I must say that I sympathised. You can't beat starting as pack leader from around eight weeks — provided that you do it right.

John Cunningham's attitude was now as if

23

Andrew was asking for his daughter's hand in marriage. Evidently he had doubts about Andrew's ability to bring a pup on from scratch – doubts that I secretly shared. But when it emerged that I am the boss of the dog unit, that was different. (He seemed to be assuming that we were a couple and to deny it would have been to upset the applecart.) What he produced was the last of his available stock because, as I feared, quite responsible people do give each other spaniel pups for Christmas. He had, in fact, been sold out but a pair of bitch pups had been booked by a man who had suddenly been offered a job in the Far East. A deposit had been forfeited, so that he could offer a good discount.

As soon as Andrew realised that the pair came within the combined contributions of us sponsors, he wanted them both. (The fact that those had been 'up to' figures quite passed him by.) Mr Cunningham, either because he didn't want to break up the pair or possibly scenting a larger cheque, encouraged him. I pointed out to Andrew that two pups would double the costs of inoculation, spaying, medication, feed, microchipping, insurance and so forth and that training two pups simultaneously is impossible and that two separately take twice as long, but all to no avail. Cunningham's business partner, Mrs Kitts (a name I associate with some very successful trial

24

results), was available. She is a vet, but I had promised to see that Andrew had a square deal. She did not seem at all worried as I checked for umbilical hernia, counted toes and examined their mouths. The blink reflex was satisfactory and I made sure that each pup responded to noises without being prompted by the other. We also met both parents and they were sound and attractive spaniels with minor awards to their credit and a Field Trial Champion only one generation back.

Before I knew it, I was writing a cheque for a very substantial sum, to cover not only the two pups but a range of food, toys and baskets that would certainly have been beyond the capacity of Andrew's car. Receipts, KC registrations and pedigrees were handed over. The two pups quickly settled down with Pippa mothering them and we set off. Andrew, who on the outward journey had shown all the signs of being smitten with me although, to do him justice, he did keep his hands to himself, now had a new outlet for his passion. The occasional snowflakes had turned into the beginning of a blizzard but as far as he was concerned the sun was blazing down. I will say that in one respect he is all there. I had mentioned the maximum budget figure at some point and he soon figured it out that there was something left in the kitty. He had my cheque for that exact amount in a trice, as a first step towards trading up his car for something more suitable for carrying his dogs around.

On the way back, I loaded him down with pearls of wisdom about how to train spaniels and his only comment was to say that he had decided to name them Honey and Spot, which I think was intended as a compliment. (The pups are both liver-and-white, but on one of them it includes the form of a perfectly round spot on the top of her head.) I don't know how much he took in, but I called at my house on the way through Edinburgh and gathered up all the dog training books that I have been collecting over the years and never consult any more. It only remains to keep all our fingers (and preferably toes as well) crossed, hoping that he profits from all this stockpiled wisdom. I left him at his door, surrounded by a whole world of doggery, grinning all over his face. I reminded him about inoculations and left him to it.

So there you are. We have provided your ex-hubby with an outlet for his energy and affections and a readymade vehicle for intro-ductions to similarly oriented people. That should keep him occupied and out of trouble. I'll try to look in on him from time to time – along with Sandy, if I can persuade him.

All the best, Honey

Chapter Three

For some months, Honey almost lost sight of Andrew Gray and such new friends as he might have acquired with the aid of the dogs, but on behalf of her old school-friend she kept her ears open. The Social Services Department advised her that Andrew was making great progress and living an orderly life. The handlers in the dog unit sometimes reported meeting him while exercising their charges in open country. They might be preoccupied with training their dogs to follow a scent, to sniff out drugs or explosives, to disarm a gunman or to catch a fleeing criminal, but none of them would have arrived in the dog unit unless they had a genuine enthusiasm for all aspects of dog training. The word was that Andrew was proceeding strictly in accordance with the manuals, teaching by reward and affection rather than by punishment and fear, and that the two young spaniels could now be sent out to hunt in absolute confidence that they would return when whistled for and each was retrieving dummies smartly and reliably, ignoring all distractions. Occasionally Andrew would play the part of the fleeing criminal in exchange for the throwing of distraction dummies.

Eventually there came a dip in the criminal activities of the citizens of Lothian and Borders. There were no murders and few serious assaults. Crimes against property were down. Even petty crime had reduced to an almost acceptable figure. The Powers That Were, of course, claimed this as a victory in their war against crime. Privately, Honey suspected that all the serious criminals had gone abroad to spend their profits and that the credit for preventing the charges of assault from becoming murder belonged rather to the skilled work of the hospitals, underfunded though they were. Whatever the real facts, she had managed almost to clear her desk.

On a fine day in June, she decided that she owed her old friend a report on Andrew's progress. In arriving at this decision, she may been influenced by mention that on the last few occasions when he had been seen by dog-handlers he had not been unaccompanied. She was on the way home after attending the investigation of an allegation of rape which had turned out, both parties agreed, to have been no more than a case of impulsive affection. It was only a small detour from her route that brought her to Andrew's house.

She had, of course, visited the house before, but that had been in midwinter and on a day of the colourless light that often precedes snow, when she was both trying to find the place and fighting a blustery wind. Even so, it had not had the forlorn and cheerless aspect of many small houses in midwinter countryside. Now the trees were in leaf, there were flowers in the gardens and wildflowers in every verge. The situation, she was surprised to note, was idyllic and she included in her next email to Poppy that:

...His house is small but it's in a more perfect situation than I remembered and much better than I expected to find within ten minutes' drive of the perimeter of Edinburgh (say an hour and a half from the city centre without using the klaxon and blue flasher, the way traffic management is going these days).

At first, I was a little concerned because where I turned off the main road a sour-looking old man came out of a cottage and looked as if for two pins he'd shake his fist at me for daring to pass by. I only hope that he doesn't push Andrew over the edge. On the other hand, he looked like the sort of neighbour who would send any intruder away with a flea in his ear.

I found Andrew's house up a hundred yards of not-too-bad farm road. You can see the tops of the farm buildings just peeping over the crest of the hill. What pasture there is held sheep rather than cattle, which makes for a peaceful and less smelly existence. Most of the land has been given over to cereal crops. Andrew has a bit of orchard, mostly apples and doing rather well. There are fields on either side and the property is backed by a mature wood. I noticed that both house and garden, despite the depredation that a couple of puppies inevitably bring, were much smarter than when I saw them last. Somebody has been painting and planting – and doing both jobs with skill as well as enthusiasm. There are flowers galore and there were birds singing. The whole atmosphere seemed happy.

The reason for the spruceness and jollity was almost immediately apparent. There's nothing like walking one or more attractive dogs for meeting people and in this instance the acquaintance had been Jackie, who is small, female, attractively chubby, genuinely blonde, definitely pretty and about ten years younger than Andrew. She had been walking her father's golden retrievers, I was told, when they met and they had clicked immediately.

It is still not clear to me whether she has moved in with him yet, but it's only a matter of time. Her manner towards him was a mixture of adoring slave and fond mother. Typical, but just what he needed. She seems to have brought with her a touch of the gaiety that he seemed to be lacking – I can imagine them playing Chase Me Charlie in and out of the house and orchard. Her widowed father farms quite a lot of the land thereabouts and after graduating from the Do-school (College of Domestic Science if you're talking pan loaf) she stayed at home to keep house for him.

When Andrew greeted me as 'Honeypot', Jackie made the connection with Honey and Spot immediately and her attitude was cool at first until she gathered that I had a husband and a career and was only visiting on behalf of his well-meaning ex-wife. (I probably made you sound like a fusspot, but you won't mind that. You wouldn't want a jealous new wife putting in the poison or trying to drive wedges between you and your former love.)

The signs and portents are auspicious. The two obviously adore each other and there can be no doubt that a certain amount of heavy breathing goes on ... and on. When I made my sudden appearance, the two were sprawled on a rug on a patch of lawn, playing with two of the prettiest young spaniels that I ever saw. You don't sprawl in a short skirt without showing everything you've got, so one may suppose that any inhibitions the relationship suffered at first are long gone.

The small house is very orderly and organised in an unmasculine manner and the kitchen has that scrubbed smell. That, I suppose, will be the Do-school background coming to the fore. The dogs have a kennel and a fenced-in run in the garden but spend most of the day in the house. Andrew has changed his car for an old Land Rover, which lends itself to renovation, a task well suited to his skills although rather hard on the hands that you used to love having run over you, as I recall. I mentioned the old man at the road-end but they both laughed and said, 'That's Mr Gloag.' Jackie added, 'He's all right when you get to know him.'

They hastened to assure me that the pups had had all their inoculations and were spayed and microchipped. They took me into the orchard, all four bubbling with enthusiasm, to demonstrate that basic obedience training had been successfully imprinted. Jackie already had some experience in dog training, so she had been able to steer him clear of the many pitfalls. She has the use of her father's dummy-launcher and I must admit that I was impressed. The pups sat to the sound of the shot, went straight out when called by name, responded to hand signals at a distance... What's more, the pups were obviously enjoying it too, which is the fundamental sign of a good relationship. (The master's attention is a reward in itself, so it's vital to praise for good behaviour and not to scold for naughtiness.) I was almost converted to springers on the spot. And the final big advantage is that she has her own certificate and a shotgun which the law will allow him to share on her father's land and in her presence, or on approved clay pigeon grounds. Training can go forward without interruption and your ex- should be contentedly occupied from here on in. They are already doing a little rabbiting and some decoying for woodpigeon. I would have said that it was much too early to introduce pups to real quarry. And so it would be for one person on his own. But with one person to shoot and a second person to control and handle the dogs, they seem to be managing well without any tendency to run-in. They hope to introduce the dogs to picking-up during the coming season. I promised to make enquiries on their behalf.

(I have been able to help in one side-issue. The firearms officer wanted to withdraw Jackie's shotgun certificate on the grounds that she was resident with an unsuitable partner. Jackie phoned me in a panic, because her shotgun is essential to their ambitions in the matter of the dogs. The firearms officer quoted a precedent in which a certificate had been withdrawn because the holder had married a spouse with a criminal record, but I was able to point out that the case had been English, the spouse's record had been serious and that the decision had been overturned on appeal.)

I just hope that I can manage my own family as brilliantly as they seem to be managing their canine one. Because – here it comes! – I am with child at last. At a very early stage, of course. I haven't even told Sandy yet, for fear of being wrapped in cotton wool. I shall leave it until I want to be wrapped in cotton wool and then I'll play that game for all it's worth. Sandy will probably want me to retire and become full-time wife and mother, but as long as we have June to be nanny as well as domestic factotum I shall continue in my determination to end up as Chief Constable (Chief Police Officer, they call most of them now). There are one or two female CPOs in England but the breakthrough hasn't been made up here yet.

Until that happy day I remain, yours, Honeypot.

Chapter Four

DI Honey Laird was lucky in her pregnancy. Morning sickness was never more than an occasional annoyance and any desires for unusual foodstuffs were easily explained away. It was therefore some time before she found it necessary to admit publicly to her condition. Her employers offered her leave, but time spent kicking her heels around the Edinburgh house while Sandy worked his cases would have been unendurable. June refused to go on holiday while her mistress was in a delicate condition and Honey refused to visit her parental home until Sandy was free to come with her. It was stalemate. She worked on.

Exactly as she had feared, her husband's immediate impulse on hearing the news, even before wetting the foetus's head, was to wrap her in cotton wool and confine her to her bed, or at least to an easy chair, until she was safely delivered. She had had the forethought to consult a gynaecologist who was famous for an attitude of *exercise is good*, *wrap the baby in a shawl and get back to work*, and she had obtained a letter advising her to live life as normal until the last minute unless any one of a set of unlikely symptoms should appear.

This forethought stood her in good stead when she took a phone-call one evening at the very beginning of October. She and Sandy were unwinding with a drink – in her case a very nearly soft drink – tangled together at one end of the big settee, while June prepared their evening meal. Pippa, the Labrador, was snoring between their feet. Honey reached impatiently for the phone, expecting a sudden call back to work or one of those maddening calls from a salesperson determined to earn a commission by selling something that nobody could possibly want. Months earlier, the Lairds had tackled the service that purports to filter out such calls, but without apparent reduction in their numbers. But the mildly American voice that came on the line was that of her friend Hazel Carpenter.

After the briefest of enquiries into health and happiness, Hazel said, 'Are you both free on Saturday?'

Barring calamities, the Laird diaries were for once both clear on Saturday, but enquiries of that nature may be the pre-cursors to a request to entertain someone unspeakably awful or to participate in some intolerably boring non-event. Hazel was not usually guilty in this respect but you never knew. 'Possibly,' Honey said.

'We're shooting that day and we wondered if you'd like to be guests. It'll be a driven day. The grouse are beginning to recover after a long neglect. They'd only sustain one drive but we've released some ex-laying hen pheasants among the whins. It may be a short day but it could be fun.'

Sandy had his ear close to hers. Honey felt him stiffen. His first impulse was to forbid any such outing, but in the face of the gynae-cologist's advice and Honey's well-known determination, he could only nod. She knew of old the questions to ask. 'Do we bring sandwiches?'

'No.'

'Pippa?'

'Yes. We're rather short of dogs.'

'Will ankle-boots do or do we need Wel-lingtons?'

'Ankle-boots will do fine. Stay to dinner. And it's a long road home for you. Stay the night if you like. We have plenty of beds.'

'That sounds wonderful. Barring riots or

the discovery of a serial killer we'll be there with bells on.' A kindly thought occurred to her. 'I know a young couple who are training a pair of spaniels. They're desperate to get some experience at beating and picking-up.' Briefly she explained about Andrew's head-wound.

'Ask them to phone,' Hazel said. 'We're short of beaters so this was going to be one of those walk-and-stand days, turnabout, but now we find that locals are going to bring wives and sweethearts along – and teenagers – so it looks like we'll get by if the two end Guns walk with the beaters each drive. Aim for nine-thirty.'

The call finished. 'You know who that was?' Honey asked.

'That was your friend with the castle, down in the Borders.'

'Hazel Carpenter. Tinnisbeck Castle. It's pretty much reduced to a large keep now but I believe it's very comfortable. It really belongs to Jeremy. It's been in his family since Noah was a lad. Jeremy's a historian.'

'I don't come the heavy husband very often, but you should have consulted me before accepting.'

'And what would you have said?'

'I'd have said "no".'

It was high time, Honey decided, that they arrived at a clear understanding as to who would make decisions about her wellbeing. 'We won't go if you don't want me to. But if I'm not fit for a stroll in the heather carrying my twenty-bore then I'm too delicate for sex. And I'll be too delicate until after our baby is born. Much too delicate.'

Sandy dropped the subject. Seven or eight months without sex were not to be endured.

June appeared in the doorway to announce that their meal was on the table. While they sipped and waited for the soup to cool, Honey said, 'Things must be looking up for the Carpenters.'

'How do you mean?'

'The last time I was there, the grouse moor was miles of ancient heather in the process of reverting to forest and they had barely enough money to fuel the central heating. Of course, Hazel buys and restores antique furniture and she may have come across a Ming chamberpot or something.'

Sandy blew on his spoon. 'Didn't his grandfather die, not very long ago?'

'Yes. But the old chap was pretty well spent up. It was all Jeremy could do to keep him in his very swish nursing home.'

'Then at least he's relieved of that burden.

Perhaps his books are selling well.'

'I doubt it,' she said. 'He writes the occasional coffee-table book but mostly the kind of textbook that pays very little at first but stays in print for ever. The antiques must be paying the bills.'

'How come you're on their guest list?'

'It's a long story. They were going abroad and they lumbered me with taking delivery of two rehomed Labradors, one of which then produced puppies all over my flat. That was Suzy. The other was Pippa. I must have told you.'

Sandy was pensive until steak, kidney and mushroom pie was served. Honey could guess what was coming. 'I still say that you shouldn't be shooting in your condition,' he said.

'It's a driven day. No more walking than a country stroll.'

'But the shock of the recoil!'

'You are going a long way over the top,' Honey said forcefully. She had no intention of being robbed of her day out. 'You know perfectly well that if I take the twenty-bore auto I could shoot it off the tip of my nose without feeling any recoil.'

There were no outbreaks of rioting and if

any serial killers had been at work they remained undiscovered. Clothes, guns and Pippa and a generous supply of cartridges were loaded and the Lairds set off early in Honey's Range Rover. The day was bright and cool. Their journey would have taken an hour with lights flashing and klaxon yodelling, but at legitimate speed and strict adherence to the Highway Code, it took nearly two hours until, just short of Tynebrook Village, they turned off into the driveway of Tinnisbeck Castle. As they neared the castle gates they overtook Andrew Gray's Land Rover and exchanged a toot for a honk.

As with Andrew's house but on a vaster scale, Honey was struck by the general improvement – not in any one item but in the air of having been cared for. Most of the outbuildings had gone centuries earlier but the keep still stood up, square and impregnable. Pointing had been renewed in the castle walls and the windows shone with fresh paint. The margin of garden fringing the castle was bright with flowers. The spread of heather reaching down to the village showed a pattern of different textures, indicating that the heather had been burned in strips for the benefit of grouse and other wildlife.

Cars were assembling on the gravel. The Lairds were introduced around. Honey already knew some of the company. Hazel knew of her dislike of being addressed as Honeypot except by her immediate family. Honey was amused to note that Hazel, being of Bostonian origin, had also felt that the abbreviated 'Honey' was too familiar and had settled instead for her full name, Honoria, carrying Honey back in her memory to her days at a Swiss finishing school.

Looking around, she could see no sign of Andrew Gray and Jackie. 'So where are all these beaters, then?' she asked Hazel.

'They start from the village. They're assembling outside the pub.'

'It won't be open, I trust.'

Hazel laughed. 'It won't open until this evening. It belongs to Ian Argyll and he's one of the Guns.'

As usual when being introduced, Honey had felt her mind going blank. However, she already knew Hazel and Jeremy. Sam Clouson, the local vet, was memorable for his bushy moustache. Keith and Molly Calder were the parents of one of her friends. An elderly man standing apart from the others but stooping cautiously to pat any dog that came within range was Henry Colebrook.

Mr Colebrook had retained a head of red hair but it was greying and his face was etched with fine lines, so she guessed his age as approaching sixty. There was a strongly built woman in heavy tweeds who could not be Ian Argyll. The thin youth looked too young to own a pub or even to be allowed inside one. So Ian Argyll had to be the thickset man in his fifties with the silver hair who was nursing over his arm a hammer gun of some age but fine quality.

For a few minutes, while Jeremy spoke over his mobile phone to the keeper, there was an interval while the Guns got to know each other. Henry Colebrook stood slightly aside, smiling whenever anyone caught his eye, but the others were asking each other after the health of friends or exchanging platitudes with new acquaintances. General opinion seemed to be that the beauty of the day would make up for any scarcity of birds. As the sun rose higher the morning chill was banished and the day came closer to shirt-sleeve weather.

Jeremy superintended the draw for numbers and then took his stand on the top step of the castle doorway and called for attention. After welcoming his guests he went on, 'You'll meet George Brightside, the keeper, later on. He's directing the beating line. I'm deputising for him in giving the usual pep talk. You're all experienced Guns so you'll know what I mean when I say don't swing through the line and anyone shooting down the line, or behaving dangerously in any other way, will be sent home. No ground game, by which I mean rabbits or hares, but if you see a fox, which I hope you won't, and if you have a safe shot, please shoot it. Do not fire at anything at all unless you can see empty land or sky behind with a safe margin around. Keep your dogs in check but mark your birds down and by all means work your dogs to pick them up later. One of us will be picking-up behind the line – please be sure that you know exactly where. No shooting after the end of the drive. It'll be marked by a series of short blasts on a whistle.

'One further point. The first birds to arrive will be the older ones. Those are the ones we want taken out. You could say that they're the reason that we're shooting the moor at all at this early stage in its reclamation. Old birds are less fertile and also take up larger territories. I know that it's easier to shoot the followers after you've been alerted by the first arrivals, but please try very hard to be ready for them and to take the leaders. In

44

view of the speed they arrive at, anyone not familiar with grouse please shoot well ahead of them or you may be knocking off the younger birds anyway.

'We have about a third of a mile to the butts. I'll take Mr Colebrook and Mrs Laird in the Land Rover. Anybody doubting their own walking ability can squeeze in with us. Otherwise you walk – or take your own car, but I warn you that the way is rough and the ruts are quite deep. On the return journey, I'll collect whoever drew Number One. Who would that be?' Sandy Laird raised his hand. 'You and I will walk on the flanks of the beating line, then. You're fit for that?'

Sandy smiled. 'I think so.'

'Who told them I was pregnant?' Honey demanded of her husband before they parted.

'It may have slipped out,' he retorted blandly.

'I wonder which of your personal habits you'd least like to have generally known.'

Sandy laughed. 'Let me think about it and I'll choose one for you.' Having had at least part of his way, he could afford to be affable.

She left Pippa with Sandy. The exercise would do them both good. She might resent Sandy's solicitude – or interference as she thought it – but to herself she admitted that struggling through heather or stumbling along a rutted track might not be the best therapy for a pregnant lady. Mr Colebrook seemed to be past the age for curling up into back seats, so she took the rear and left him to be helped into the comparative luxury of the front. They bounced along the track. During the intervals between boulders and potholes and while the motion was almost steady, she found herself looking at the back of his head. His hair might be greying but his faint stubble still held a glint of red.

Traces remained of the original butts but temporary butts had been made from wooden pallets threaded with heather. They found their places and waited. It was a long wait but Honey found plenty to interest her. The day remained clear and, for October, warm. The view of the moor, the village, the nearer hills and far beyond was spectacular. As long as she kept very still, the wildlife went about its regular business around her. The beaters had already moved to the edge of the moor and she saw them string out over a wide front and begin their march through the heather. Butterflies were making a comeback and there were young rabbits playing in the sunshine until a buzzard sailed over. She could hear grouse. She checked behind her but Hazel, who was acting as picker-up, was well out of dangerous range.

The beating line was well handled. It came slowly, moving birds towards the Guns. There was a broad variety of dogs but they were under control. The line closed as it neared. The Guns were at the head of a depression in the ground, too shallow to be called a valley, and the beating line was closing in, to funnel the birds from a broad front onto the shorter line of Guns.

Suddenly there were grouse in the air, two parties of three or four. Pulses quickened and mouths went dry. The grouse seemed to come slowly and then, suddenly, they were rushing at the line of Guns, flicking over and gone. There was a rattle of shots. Honey had forgotten the amazing speed of them, nearly three times the speed of a pheasant, and she was caught out. She fired her twenty-bore once and missed behind. Sandy, walking on the flank, also fired once but he had the advantage of the extra time that it took for a bird to curl back. His grouse tumbled into the heather and Pippa did a retrieve. One bird was down behind the line of butts.

There was never a solid flush but for twenty minutes a thin trickle of birds came over. Henry Colebrook was in the butt next to Honey and she noticed that he was shooting well and with all proper attention to the rules of safety. The Guns adjusted the speed of their swings and a few birds fell. By the whistle for the end of the drive, eleven birds were down and the beaters brought three more. 'And nearly all old birds,' Jeremy said with satisfaction.

Pippa came with a rush, relieved to be reunited with her mistress but still exhilarated by the chance to fulfil the destiny for which she had been bred and trained. She twined round Honey's legs and then threatened to jump up. Honey pushed her down. 'All right,' she said fondly. 'So you enjoyed yourself. And you did well. Big deal!' Pippa settled for leaning against her mistress's legs and panting.

Hazel arrived, also panting, with her Suzy at heel. 'One flew on and then dropped suddenly,' she said. 'I think it's in that copse of silver birch but Suzy can't find it.'

The beaters had arrived and were mingling with the Guns. Honey saw Henry Colebrook exchange a glance with one of the beaters but neither seemed ready for conversation. Andrew and Jackie were grinning happily. Jackie touched Hazel's arm. 'May we try for the lost bird? Please?'

Hazel smiled. 'Go on, then.' She looked around. 'Tea, coffee or cold drinks in front of the castle, everybody,' she said.

Mary Kershaw, the castle housekeeper, had laid out a long table with a white cloth and small snacks to go with the drinks. Guns and beaters mingled in the bonhomie unique to such occasions. To primitive man the hunt and the feast that followed were the high points in his existence. Modern mankind still celebrates great occasions with a feast, but those who have never known the zest of gathering their own meat in company, Honey thought, were missing the cream. Andrew and Jackie returned while drinks were being taken. The pair were beaming all over their faces. The spaniels also seemed to be smiling. Andrew held up the missing grouse. 'It had legged it along the ditch,' he said. 'Honey followed it up.'

There was a murmur of appreciation. Hazel looked at Honoria. 'Your namesake's wiped Suzy's eye for her,' she said.

All the dogs in the beating line had worked hard in the heather and most lay down for a rest, but Spot and Honey went the rounds, receiving praise and titbits. Their manners were attractive, so they were treated generously. They were inordinately fond of peppermints.

Behind the castle, a long crest was crowned with broken ground. Here there was no heather but gorse, rocks and broom with sudden patches of grass. Ex-laying hen pheasants had been released four months earlier, as soon as their duty was done for the year, so that there would be mature birds early in the season. The Carpenters managed to detach everybody from the refreshments and a quick drive was held before lunch. The buffet meal that followed was held in the echoing entrance hall of the keep, Guns and beaters again mingling cheerfully and somehow avoiding the dogs underfoot. The keepering was praised. Everyone, Jeremy explained, had mucked in at the previous winter's moor-burning and it had developed into a beery barbecue and barndance.

Strong drinks were available but Jeremy was careful to see that nobody over-indulged. Those dogs that did not spend the interval at rest were busily scrounging petting or scraps.

Jeremy was soon urging the Guns to move. Sandy was asked to look for Mr Colebrook and found him outside, chatting to Hannah

Phillipson while feeding peppermints to Andrew's spaniels. The keeper, George Brightside, was seventy-six according to Jeremy although he looked not a day over fifty. He agreed that the beaters could rest for a few minutes more, which was generally agreed to be fair, considering that they were doing the hardest work and had the shortest distance to travel.

The two drives of the afternoon went by in a blur. The pheasants flew well, but compared to the grouse they were as cargo planes compared to military jets. The Guns treated them accordingly. The day ended with enough birds to provide a brace apiece for everybody, beaters included. The bag was laid out and duly admired.

The party broke up, with much handshaking and tips to the keeper. Sandy and Honey were staying overnight. Andrew and Jackie had accepted the dinner invitation but decided to leave for home immediately thereafter, for the sake of the spaniels. Mr Colebrook, the only other guest with a long road to travel, had declined both invitations with effusive thanks and left as soon as good manners permitted.

That evening, from a bedroom at Tinnisbeck Castle, Honey emailed to Poppy:

51

Spot and my namesake were quite brilliant and much admired by everyone. If they go on gathering titbits at the same pace they'll end up as fat as pigs, but I think you can stop worrying about your ex. His relationship with Jackie appears to be as strong as ever and the two now have a common obsession that will act as a bond and keep them both occupied. I can envisage them being in demand for beating and picking-up for almost half of every year. It won't bring in much money and they'll probably get sick of the taste of pheasant, but the therapy seems to be dragging his mental processes up towards total recovery.

The only danger I can see is that, if she is attached to him by her mothering instinct, she may cool if he recovers enough of his marbles to becomes less dependent; but my guess is that she worships him for the hero she thinks he once was. And a good thing too! Jeremy Carpenter would probably point to a historical tradition for rewarding the returning hero with maidens, which may not have been PC in the light of today's attitudes but I dare say was enjoyed by both parties and must have gone far to encourager les autres.

Chapter Five

The next day being Sunday and with no duty looming, Honey had promised herself an easy day to make up for all the tiredness induced by fresh air and exercise, and the stiffness after much use of muscles that saw little use during the usual day's routine. She lay for as long as she dared but she knew that if she dallied any longer Pippa would start making the moaning noise that signalled her displeasure at breakfast being delayed. Then everyone else would get up and try not to seem aggrieved for the remainder of the morning.

Mobile phones are unwelcome on shoots, demanding attention as they always do at the very moment when everyone's attention should be on the birds, and she had left hers in the car the previous day; so in order to catch any urgent messages she had left it on charge but switched on overnight. She had just dragged herself out of bed, hauling along with her a bump which, while not yet noticeable to anyone else, was beginning to seem to her like a sack of potatoes hung around her waist, when her phone began its little tune. The English fraud case in which Sandy had previously had only a peripheral interest had now been found to have an origin in Scotland where also three of the four major participants were living, and he had therefore been required to take over the reins. Obviously the call would be for him and she said as much. Sandy pointed out that he had his own cellphone with him, to which Honey retorted that his phone was not switched on. Grumbling, he roused himself, reached out and answered the call. It was for her, which put a severe if momentary dent in the marital bliss.

On the line was Andrew's Jackie. (They didn't know her surname at the time but it turned out to be Fulson.) Something supremely terrible had happened, but whenever she tried to explain it over the phone she choked on the words. Help and comfort were required immediately if not much, much sooner. Honey said that she would come along as soon as she had had some breakfast, which brought on another bout of weeping. From it, she gathered that there was no time for eating but that if such irrelevancies as food were really necessary at a time like this, Jackie would make her some bloody breakfast but do hurry!

Honey explained all this to Sandy while hurling herself into some clothes but he seemed to have gone back to sleep. He awoke enough to say for God's sake to go, quietly, and he would beg a lift home from somebody or, at a pinch, be very naughty and summon a Traffic car. He was asleep again before she left the bedroom. She gave Pippa a few seconds in the outdoors for reasons of comfort and hygiene before harrying her into the back of the Range Rover.

The roads were clear at that hour of a Sunday morning and the weather was fine. She was able to drive fast while still wondering what the fuss was about. Andrew could not have died in the night, because she had heard his voice in the background. Pippa, robbed for the moment of her breakfast, moaned all the way. In less time than she would have admitted to, she was at the door of *Thack an Raip* – the name of their cottage and very old Scots language for 'home comforts'. While still ten minutes off, Honey phoned to report her imminent arrival. Jackie, on the phone, sounded very slightly calmer. Honey was there in another five minutes but she was none too soon, because Jackie was on the point of frying a major mixed grill whereas all Honey ever took in the morning was cereal and toast. Jackie was, it seemed, trying to keep busy. She and Andrew were both grey and shaking with nerves and grief.

While Honey breakfasted on her least favourite cereal, Jackie toasted what could only be called a doorstep of bread and Pippa enjoyed a breakfast borrowed from Spot and Honey, Jackie and Andrew blurted out their story. It emerged in no sort of order but when Honey had managed to make sense of it, it amounted to this. They had left Tinnisbeck Castle for home yesterday at about eight p.m. They had fed the pups and been in bed well before midnight, pleasantly tired from fresh air and exercise. They heard nothing during the night but when Jackie looked out of their bedroom window in the dawn she saw that the gate of the run was open. Her frantic dash up the garden (in the nude, Honey gathered) revealed that both pups were missing. The padlock had been removed forcibly.

Pausing to put some clothes on, they had dashed around their favourite dog-walks, calling and whistling, but with no result. When Honey asked whether they had called the police they pointed out that, as far as they were concerned, she *was* the police. She called the local station (five miles away) and left a message on an answering machine. So much, she thought, for that. Probably her call had just missed the local constable, who had left to answer a call about the finding of stray spaniels – whether dead or alive she could only guess and hope.

Andrew was building up a head of steam and could do little more than recite what he would do to the villains if he ever caught up with them. Jackie, however, now that the presence of help and support was having a calming effect, turned out to have a head on her shoulders. She pointed out to him that he might only be talking himself into trouble and it would be more to the point to expend his energy on getting the dogs back. Honey explained that, pending the hoped-for call from the local bobby or some helpful neighbour, they should start the process of a wider search. For this, they would need an email facility, preferably with a scanner.

The household did not possess a computer. Jackie dashed off up to the farm in Andrew's Land Rover to borrow equipment from her father. Andrew was set to bustling about, trying to find the best photographs that they had of the spaniels. Meanwhile Honey took a look at the scene of the crime. The padlock looked as though it had been removed with bolt-cutters. The only other clue was a tyre-print in what had been mud but was drying hard. Once she could be sure that it did not belong to her car or theirs, she demanded a packet of Polyfilla from Andrew and made a cast. It was almost certainly wasted effort but the fact that something was being done continued to exert a calming influence.

Farming was becoming more and more high-tech and Mr Fulson was well equipped for it. Jackie came back with what turned out to be her father's spare computer, a rather dated model but with adequate power and its own modem. She had also obtained a short-term loan of his scanner. Honey fed in her own address and password and they were ready to go. One of the handlers at the dog unit had a home phone number that was memorable by virtue of the repetition of digits. She called him and he was able to look out the email address of the Kennel Club.

The slickest *modus operandi* usually requires two people, one on the phone finding out email addresses or phone numbers and the other at the computer. This may need two phone lines, but *Thack an Raip* was not so well provided; she gave Andrew her mobile, sat Jackie down at the computer and told her to email details and pictures to the Kennel Club, making sure to tell them that the pups were microchipped and spayed and wearing collars with identifying tags on them. At the same time, she was to ask the KC to notify all dog clubs in Scotland or to furnish email addresses. Then she was to email the governing body of the shooting clubs and syndicates, letting it be known that news of the sudden appearance of any year-old liver-and-white pups might result in a reward. After that, she could work through all the vets in the Yellow Pages.

Those tasks, she thought, should at least keep the pair occupied and give them a feeling that they were doing something potentially useful. She had no great hope of a positive result. One stolen dog is very like any other and if the new handler had a credible story it would take a determined acquaintance to question it. But the distress of the young couple was so total that she had to try. She left them to it and hurried stumbling down the farm road.

Mr Gloag was already at his door, looking

as sour as ever. She supposed that an old man living alone might be expected to let order and hygiene slip a bit, but on approaching to within a few yards she was not inclined to come any closer. His face was much wrinkled by the passage of time and, to be fair, probably hard work as well; but she suspected that his morning wash had been a pass with a damp cloth, merely removing dirt from the ridges but passing over the furrows.

He asked who she was and what she wanted. Neither question was couched in polite terms; nor did he seem interested in getting an answer. It was not her habit to throw her constabulary weight around, preferring to achieve her ends by guile, charm and, if necessary, a little sex appeal. But this seemed to be a case where sex appeal had ceased to be appropriate. Perhaps a little bullying was called for. She moved to be upwind of him in the slight morning breeze, held up her identification and introduced herself, laying stress on the *Detective Inspector*. In ominous tones she added, 'It seems that you've been a bad boy.' Not many people have consciences so clear as to resist that gambit.

It produced a good but unexpected result.

He blanched under the dirt. 'It's no ma blame if yon limmer gaes aroon in the scud,' he said.

That gave her just the clue she needed. A glance over her shoulder assured her that he could not have seen Jackie's dash to the kennel and back from his own premises. She pointed out that as a Peeping Tom he could be prosecuted and placed on the Sex Offenders Register. She did not actually say that there had been complaints, but the implication may have been there. She warned him against any repetition of such behaviour and then said that the matter might go no further if he could help in regard to the loss of two young dogs from his neighbours.

Her guess must have been a good one. He was tumbling over himself to be helpful. He invited her to search his cottage, but nothing would have tempted her over that threshold. She did peep through the cleaner parts of his windows and poke through his outbuildings without sight or sound of a dog. His help extended to answering a few questions, and here he turned out to be more intelligent than she had given him credit for. He had been woken in the night by the sound of a vehicle passing by. It had been a diesel, he could tell by the sound and the smell that filtered through his window, and it might have been about the size of a Land Rover. It had not been an automatic – he recognised the sound of manual gear changing. It had gone past Andrew's cottage and on towards the farm.

There had been a slight frost and in the calm air the sounds had carried clearly. The vehicle had gone on, slightly uphill, to the farmyard, where it had turned. The engine had stopped and he had supposed that it had reached its destination. To his surprise, about five minutes later he heard what seemed to be the same engine re-start right outside his door and the vehicle had driven off towards Edinburgh. The explanation was obvious. Rather than rouse Andrew and Jackie by stopping at the door, the thief had driven up to the farmyard and freewheeled back to the kennel. He had cut off the pad-lock, transferred the spaniels to the vehicle and freewheeled again on the slight downslope to the road. Spaniels often bark at a passing fox or badger, so a little noise from Spot and Honey might not have awoken the humans. On the other hand, the fact that Jackie and Andrew had passed a peaceful night might suggest that the thief was somebody known to the dogs. It also seemed probable that the thief knew the layout of the farm roads.

She was taking her leave of the unpleasant Mr Gloag with a final warning about voyeurism, when a smart little police car turned in off the road. She had not expected her answerphone message to be answered at all on a Sunday, let alone so promptly, and her satisfaction was increased when she recognised the neat, uniformed figure of the driver. PC Webber had been a newly fledged constable in Newton Lauder when she was first assigned there. He had made a serious mistake, allowing a murderous rapist to slip through his fingers, and the Big Bugs had wanted him for a scapegoat. The man had been recaptured only a few minutes later and the mistake had originated with somebody further up the hierarchy. Honey had put her career on the line, fought for him and saved his bacon and he knew it. His face lit up when he saw her. She got in beside him for the short run up to *Chez* Andrew.

'What's it all about, Inspector?' he asked as he drew up. He was one of the few subordinates who she would have allowed to call her Honey, or even Honeypot, but he had respect.

She brought him up to speed with the dognapping and what had so far been done about it. He took it down in laborious short-hand. They went inside and made introductions. PC Webber announced his approval of the steps so far taken. He could hardly do otherwise faced with a Detective Inspector on the same Force, even if he had not still been showing the signs of believing that the sun rose and set at her command. Andrew had produced a very lively photograph of the two dogs and Jackie had scanned it and included it in a carefully worded email. They were now working their way down the list of vets, but that could wait. Very few vets' offices would be open on a Sunday.

When she had them all seated around the kitchen/dining table, Honey said, 'There are two main possibilities. One, somebody on yesterday's shoot fell for the dogs or saw the chance of a quick profit and followed them home.'

'That could be it.' Jackie said. 'I was driving, because Andy had wanted to be free to have a drink. And there seemed to be lights in my mirror, a long way back, all the way home. Of course, I couldn't be sure that it was the same car all the time,' she added.

'Of course not. The other possibility is that somebody around here took them. Maybe to sell. It's becoming a more common crime. It's less likely that somebody around here wants to keep them. You'd have been bound to run across them at some time.'

Jackie was looking at her intensely. 'There's something you don't want to say. Isn't there?'

It had to be said. 'They could have been taken out of spite, by somebody who hates one or both of you.'

'In which case,' Jackie said slowly, 'they'd probably kill them. That's what you didn't want to say, isn't it?' Honey nodded. (Andrew was making a sound indicating inner turmoil.) 'But if it was spite, surely it would have been easier just to poison them where they were. And it would have hit us harder.'

She had a point, but you never know how a vengeful mind will work. It might well have reasoned that uncertainty and imagination might have hurt more and for longer than mere death, but Honey decided not to mention that point.

'But who could hate either of us that much?' Jackie asked.

On the spur of the moment it was difficult to imagine anyone hating Jackie. 'No discarded boyfriends?'

'Certainly not! Andrew was my first and only.'

'What about the man whose jaw you broke?' Honey asked Andrew.

Andrew looked at her vaguely. 'Don't think so,' he said. 'We've had a pint together since then. He was friendly. Apologetic, we both were. I shouldn't have lost my rag and I told him so.'

'It would still be worth checking on his whereabouts last night,' she suggested to Constable Webber.

He nodded. 'I can go and do that now. He's only a few miles away.' He hurried out and she heard the little car drive off.

'Who else have you had a punchup with?' she asked Andrew.

'Nobody. I swear it.'

'Not even a shouting match?'

'No.'

'He never shouts,' Jackie said.

That had the ring of truth. Even in his wrath, Andrew was softly spoken. 'Just in case it was somebody who was on yesterday's shoot,' Honey said, 'we'd better know more about the guests.' She took back her phone and called Tinnisbeck Castle.

Hazel answered the phone. Sandy, she said, was at breakfast. Honey had already said all the proper things about their hospitality but she said them again as quickly as possible. When Hazel heard about the stolen dogs, she was horrified. She could imagine her own desolation if Suzy should go missing. She quite understood that the fullest information about the other guests might prove helpful. 'We're just in the middle of a very early lunch,' she said. 'More of a brunch, really. We're planning to go to Edinburgh this afternoon. We'll almost pass the door. Would it help if we called in around two o'clock?'

Honey said that it would and she gave her directions. Hazel promised to give Sandy a lift home. Honey thanked her and disconnected. At least that solved the problem of getting Sandy safely back to Edinburgh. Cross off one problem.

There was one other theory to be eliminated. 'When you did your search this morning,' she said, 'was the frost still on the ground?'

They both nodded. 'We were studying it for useful traces,' Jackie said.

'You went all round the farm?' she asked, as casually as she could manage.

'First thing,' Andrew said. 'There was no sign that they'd been there. The frost was unmarked.'

Jackie was, as they say, sharp enough to cut herself. She turned white. 'You think that my father could have taken the dogs? Why would he? As a ruse? To drive a wedge between us?'

'It's a possibility.'

Jackie had lost all her colour but she stayed calm. 'No it is not,' she said. 'My father has no objection to Andrew, who helps him out whenever he's short-handed, though Dad did say once that he'd prefer that we got properly married – which we plan to do in the spring, by the way. But we went right round the farm anyway, in case the dogs had wandered up there. There were no marks in the frost and no answer to our whistles except a bark from Dad's dogs. They're kennelled in a shed.'

Honey, for once, was at a loss. She didn't know whether to apologise or to say *That's good* or *What a pity!* Instead, she dropped the subject and let them go back to their emails. She borrowed the whistle to which the spaniels had been accustomed. Her boots had been in the car throughout a frosty night and putting her warm feet into them was misery, but she gritted her teeth and suffered. She took Pippa for a walk around the immediate fields, calling and whistling. Once again, it was almost certainly wasted effort but it was better than sitting still in a house that reeked of desperation.

Deep inside, she was as upset as the young owners were. A disaster, she thought wryly, can hurt a third party more than the victim because the stranger is more impotent; the sufferer may at least fight back. She tried to detach her mind and take comfort from the bright, crisp day and Pippa's delight in being out in it. There were tree strips between the fields. The leaves were already down from the birches, but the other hardwoods were glowing with autumn colours. There were berries in the hedge bottoms and squirrels overhead.

She turned her steps in the direction of the farmhouse – a substantial building and far too large for one man if, as she supposed, Jackie's father was now alone. A man was crossing the farmyard with two dogs at heel. He paused and the dogs sat immediately. Pippa did the same after one disdainful glance. The man was in working clothes but from his bearing she guessed, correctly as it turned out, that he was Mr Fulson, Jackie's father.

'I've had a damn good look through the

outbuildings,' he said. 'I'm just away to search further. There's one or two places a dog could fall or get shut in. I'm not hopeful, mind. I could see one dog getting into that sort of trouble, but not two. Or they could have picked up something poisoned and be in need of the vet.' He was a pleasant looking man, well spoken and, apart from a balding head, not showing much sign of the passing years.

'I'll help all I can,' Honey said.

'Aye. Do that. Yon lassie of mine's in a rare taking. No doubt her young man's taking it hard?'

'Very hard.'

'He would.' Mr Fulson nodded sadly. 'That's a good man she's got there. Maybe he's a bit slow, but that's a wound he got in the service of his country and it won't have done his genes any harm. Not that I approved of the Iraq war, mind, but no way was it his fault. His duty was to go where he was sent. And I'd just as soon she took up with someone who lives close by. They've been good for each other. I'd hate to see anything tear them apart.'

Honey resumed her patrol. There was no response to her shouts and whistles. She had to abandon her efforts when, from a distance, she saw a Porsche at the door of *Thack an Raip*. She composed her face and strode back across the fields.

Chapter Six

The Porsche, as she expected, had brought Jeremy and Hazel Carpenter but not Sandy. Hazel explained that they had dropped Sandy at home at his request. Honey refused to be hurt or disappointed. She quite understood that Sandy had his own life to lead; he might also be unsure of her movements and wary of being stranded somewhere in the surprisingly empty countryside that can still be found around Edinburgh. But with so much supercharged emotion on the loose, she could well have done with his advice and the comfort of his presence. It was impossible to remain detached while the sufferers were young people for whom one had been developing a certain fondness.

The cottage was in the throes of modernisation and decoration. Paint pots stood where vases of flowers might have been expected. Most of the dingy wallpaper had been stripped, leaving white stripes like stalactites, but the Carpenters were unperturbed. They had lived through similar disruption as the castle was brought up to date. They accepted chairs at the kitchen table. Jackie and Andrew sat with hands tightly linked but they looked at Honey, who realised that she had been elected spokesman – which, she decided, was one of the penalties of official status.

'Somebody came in the night,' she said. 'A diesel vehicle, about the size of a Land Rover. The padlock was cut off the gate of the run, apparently with bolt-cutters. The dogs may be running loose but this looks more like the deliberate taking of particular dogs, for reward or out of desire.'

This was old news to Andrew and Jackie, yet Honey saw them both flinch.

'But that's awful! I can see how it might look,' Hazel said. In her distress, her faint Bostonian accent became stronger. She ran her fingers through her always unruly hair. Her face had no pretension to beauty but it was pleasantly animated and as long as her hair was dressed she managed somehow to please the eye. With her hair in unintentionally comical disarray the effect was clownish. 'From your viewpoint, I mean,' she said, sniffing. 'Those two very pretty little dogs, working so well and being admired by everybody, anyone might lust after them.'

She smiled suddenly, bringing sunshine to her otherwise undistinguished face and relieving it for a moment of its comical expression. 'I do. I'd kill to have them. And all right, so obviously it makes one of your best starting points. But I think I can save you a lot of time here. I'll phone Ian Argyll. You met him yesterday. In theory, Jeremy's the laird. Ian considers himself still a servant of the castle, but in fact he's the boss of everything for miles around. He's related to everybody and he runs the village like a benevolent despot.'

'We can vouch for him, absolutely,' Jeremy put in. 'I've known him for most of my life. There's no doubting his honesty. He doesn't need money and he doesn't give a damn about dogs. We offered him one of Suzy's pups, as a gift. He looked at the litter, said they were "Awfu' bonny", then turned away and went on talking about replacement windows.'

'I'll call him now,' Hazel said. There was a faintly interrogatory note in her voice and she waited for a second or two before taking out her own phone. Honey knew the value in some cases of getting as many of the public as possible motivated to help. Hazel keyed in two digits and waited. Soon, Ian's

74

deep voice could be heard, distorted by the smallness of the telephone's speaker. 'Ian,' said Hazel, 'you remember those two spaniels that came with the young couple, the ones who performed so well. The dogs were stolen during the night. It's possible that somebody followed them home. In a diesel vehicle, if that helps. Would you mention it to all your aunts and cousins? Get any news that you can and make sure that you hear if anybody has suddenly come by one or more new dogs or some money.' She listened for a moment. The faint voice could be heard in the room, but without words. 'No, of course we don't think that any of your relatives stole the dogs, but somebody may have heard something and you could all keep your ears wide open. That pub of yours is the hotbed of all the gossip for miles around. We'd be very grateful. Thanks, Ian.' She disconnected. 'Who else?'

'Henry Colebrook,' Jeremy said.

Hazel nodded. 'Ah, now here you find us at a disadvantage. You probably know more about him than we do.' Andrew and Jackie looked puzzled. 'Well, he lives somewhere near here.'

'This is the first we ever knew of it,' Jackie

said. 'We met him for the first time at the shoot but without ever knowing that he was a neighbour. Andrew only moved here quite recently, when the tenant who had been here since his aunt left him the house suddenly left. And then he was a bit of a hermit until I came along. And I'd been at boarding school rather a lot until not long ago. And I went on a lot of school trips and stayed with friends. Dad was always afraid that I might find it dull, cooped up on the farm, but I don't. And I didn't. Then, since I met Andrew, we've been rather pre-occupied with each other. And the dogs.' Her voice broke and her eyes filled with tears again. Andrew put an arm round her and whispered in her ear. She shook her head. 'No, I'm all right,' she whispered.

After an uncomfortable pause, Hazel said, 'He did seem a little surprised when we mentioned that you and he had adjacent postcodes. Well, I'll tell you what little we know. It was this way. We came back from the Eastern Med on a cruise ship after Jeremy's last research trip. Jeremy backs his early history with a lot of archaeology. Well, he'd worked hard in rough conditions and we felt that we owed ourselves a holiday. Mr Colebrook was a fellow passenger, travelling on his own, and he was put at our table, so we became pally enough to exchange drinks and chat a bit. He was very quiet and not too forthcoming, but that's rather the way Jeremy is for most of the time, so we liked him all the better for that. We were already planning yesterday's shoot, to get at the pheasants before they all wandered off and to thin out the older grouse, but like you we don't know a lot of people. Jeremy had been writing and researching constantly to keep his granddad in his top-of-the-range nursing home until the old man died; I'm a comparatively recent arrival and we live a reclusive sort of life. So when we found that he was an experienced shot and lived within driving distance, we invited him. And I must say that he kept his end up. He turned out to be a good shot and when he forgot to feel sorry for himself he could keep up with the best of us, walking.'

'That's a bit unfair,' Honey protested. 'About being sorry for himself, I mean. Arthritis tends to ease off a bit when you get moving, or so my ageing relatives tell me. Then you stiffen up when you sit or stand around.'

'I'll give him the benefit of the doubt. I hope I never find out for myself. Anyway, he sold up his business a few years ago,' said Jeremy. 'Since then, he's been living a rather solitary existence. He said that his life at the head of a chain of supermarkets, with filling stations and delivery services and all kind of side interests, had been one long process of listening to people who couldn't express themselves clearly and who then got indignant when misunderstandings developed. He preferred to retreat into books and music.'

Honey knew exactly how the old man had felt. She was usually very sociable but sometimes, usually when defence lawyers had been belabouring her, she wished that she too could withdraw from the world, seeing nobody but Sandy. 'He doesn't sound a very likely suspect,' she said. 'Who else can't Ian vouch for?'

'The Calders,' Andrew said, breaking his long silence.

'Keith and Molly?' Honey said. 'I know them both. I can vouch for them absolutely. Keith might cheat the taxman but he wouldn't stoop to dognapping. He's comfortably off; and he knows that I know his daughter well, so I can very easily find out if any new dogs have passed through his hands. Who else?'

'There was Sam Clouson, the local vet,' said Jeremy. 'He seems all right but we don't exactly know him except for his attending to Suzy and the pups. He must be making a good income–'

'And spending it,' Hazel said.

'–all right, and spending it. He has a bit of a reputation. Girls, some of them quite young. He could be paying maintenance all over the place.'

Honey shook her head. 'We've said it before and I'll say it again, a well-trained spaniel can be valuable, but a spayed bitch without her pedigree does not have much market value.'

A well-trained working gundog can fetch a few hundred,' said Jeremy. 'That can be a lifesaver to a desperate man. His wife holds most of the money in that family – she was the daughter of a merchant banker – and she cracks the whip now and again. About money, mostly – I don't think she puts as high a value on fidelity. But I can't see him putting a good practice and a lucrative marriage at risk by chancing a very damaging lawsuit or a prosecution.'

'All that you've said suggests that he'd have no reason to go in for dognapping,' his wife pointed out.

Jeremy nodded. 'Let's move on, then. Hannah Phillipson.'

'She was probably a mistake,' Hazel said. 'She lives about eight or ten miles west of the castle, with a clinging, fluffy sort of woman. They have a smallholding, run a few sheep and grow some vegetables. They try to be self-sufficient. They also have a bit of a craft workshop and Hannah does dressmaking and things. She made up the new curtains for us.'

Andrew emerged momentarily from his despond. 'Are they lesbians?' he asked curiously.

'Who knows? They would deny it,' said Hazel. 'To be fair, there is a man around somewhere. It may be a *ménage à trois*. I met them at a meeting to protest about a proposed wind farm. That led to the new curtains. Then, when Hannah started hinting, I couldn't turn my back without seeming rude. Anyway, there was nothing wrong with her. I don't know why men get uptight about women in the shooting field,' she added. 'I thought the days of that sort of sexist attitude were long gone.'

'Don't you believe it!' Honey said. 'I've never understood why some men resent seeing women shooting.'

'I'll explain,' said Jeremy. 'Forget about shooting being a male preserve and man being the hunter. The fact is that the presence of ladies makes it very awkward and uncomfortable for the man who needs a pee.'

'We'll have to put up some canvas screens. Anyway, Hannah shot well, behaved politely and thanked everybody afterwards.' Hazel paused and a slight frown drifted over her brow. 'She knew the drill all right and yet she undertipped George Brightside, the keeper. That suggests a shortage of cash. My guess is that she shoots mostly for the pot. I slipped her an extra pheasant out of a sort of pity. I think that's all, except for my nephew, the skinny boy who never spoke much. I can vouch for him and anyway I know where he was last night.'

While she spoke, there had been the sound of a small car. PC Webber was back at the door. Jackie hopped up to let him in. Honey introduced him around and explained his presence.

'I had a de'il of a job finding your mannie,' he said. 'I tracked him down in the end. Then I had to go find the lady who was his alibi. But it checked out in the end. He was in bed.'

81

Honey was still busily recording the discussion. She looked up. 'What about the beating line? Which of them made a fuss of the dogs?'

'All of them,' Jackie said. 'Except Mrs Clouson, the vet's wife. She doesn't like dogs much.'

'Most of the rest were villagers and connected to Ian Argyll, one way or another,' Jeremy said. 'We can leave them to him. There was Johnny Cruikshank. We don't know much about him – he lives at the smallholding, but what his status is there I wouldn't know, probably wouldn't want to. Miss Phillipson brought him.'

'But he was nice,' Jackie protested.

Honey refrained from pointing out that niceness was not proof of innocence. 'We'll look at him,' she said. 'If he's innocent we may as well get him out of the way.'

Jackie nodded reluctantly. 'Well, all right. But I was much less taken with the man working what looked like a spaniel collie cross. The rather dark, rough sort of man with stubble and a woollen cap. His dog was good, though.'

'That would be Pat Kerr,' Jeremy said. 'We don't know much about him. He lives somewhere in or close to the village and I've seen him driving a van. He was one of George Brightside's first recruits. If George can't vouch for him, he'll certainly need to be looked at. He and Cruikshank seemed to be acquainted.'

'I think that's all,' Hazel said, 'except for the four teenagers, and I think that they all came with Ian Argyll.'

Honey put down her pencil and stretched her cramped fingers. Since her promotion, her hand had lost its cunning and her shorthand had almost deserted her. 'Before we start galloping off in all directions,' she said, 'I think that Jackie should see whether your emails have produced anything. I suppose Mr Argyll will phone as soon as he's learned anything. But,' she shifted her eyes to PC Webber, 'you could check whether any strays have been found.'

'Yes, of course.' Jackie pulled the computer closer and switched it on. PC Webber got up, intending to use his radio from outside. They were interrupted by a rap on the door. Andrew jumped up and went to answer it. They heard a voice say, 'Is the local Bobby here? I phoned the station and I was told...'

Andrew stepped back and a man appeared in the doorway, his head of red hair glowing in the sunlight against the dark room.

Despite herself, Honey drew in her breath. Webber was still standing and it was clear that the newcomer was the taller. 'I'm Daniel Colebrook,' he said. 'Are you here about my father?'

'What about your father?'

His face fell. 'Oh. I thought you must know. It seems that he never arrived home last night.' Daniel Colebrook looked round and realised that the small room was inhabited. 'Perhaps we could speak outside?'

'Maybe that would be best.'

'One moment,' Honey said briskly. 'There's no mistaking who you are. When you came in at the door I thought, against the light, that it was your father coming in. I see now that you're younger. Your father is Henry Colebrook, who was shooting at Tinnisbeck Castle yesterday, right? We were all present there, except for Constable Webber. We may have something to offer. What can you tell us?'

Daniel hesitated. 'This is Detective Inspector Laird,' Allan Webber said.

'Ah.'

Andrew brought forward the last unoccupied chair and the newest comer settled onto it. Honey noticed that he had the same square jaw as his father, the slightly Roman nose and blue eyes set slightly close together, but his face was broader across the cheekbones and his ears protruded slightly.

Honey introduced him around. 'Now,' she said. 'Begin at the beginning. For the record, your father is...?'

'As you said, Henry Colebrook. Of Moonside House. It's just over the hill past the farm from here. I live in Lasswade. My older brother, Vernon, lives just a mile or two away in Corrie Cottage. You know it?' Allan Webber nodded. 'He phoned me this morning. Maggie McLaghan, my father's housekeeper, had phoned him. My father isn't there this morning and there's no sign that he slept there last night. That's unheard-of for him. Vernon phoned Tinnisbeck Castle but didn't get an answer, so he was going to go there while I came here.'

'Vernon's out of luck,' Jeremy said. 'Does he have a mobile phone?'

'His was stolen just the other day. He never used it much anyway.'

'Then you've no way of saving him a long and fruitless journey. Our housekeeper's gone visiting so the castle's empty. Your father certainly isn't there. He decided not to stay to dinner last night. He said it would make him later than he liked to be and that he'd probably call in for a quick meal at one of the hotels much nearer home.'

'That sounds like him. For a formerly successful businessman he's very shy.'

'You resemble him strongly,' Honey said.

'In all except the shyness.' Daniel smiled, increasing the resemblance. 'We all do – Vernon perhaps more than I do. We have a younger brother as well, Leo, but his resemblance to Dad isn't quite so strong. He takes rather after our late mother. I know which are Dad's favourite hotels, I'd better go and phone them.'

'Now, hold on a minute,' Honey said. 'Your father hasn't been missing for long enough to be officially a missing person, and I don't think that wasting a few minutes of your time will do anything other than give him a chance to turn up of his own accord. Does your father have any worries?'

Daniel looked surprised at the very idea. 'Not that I can imagine. He lives modestly and quietly on an annuity and a few investments. His health is generally good.'

'Could he have any enemies?'

'I doubt it very much. If he does, it would have to be somebody from years ago. Since he retired, he doesn't meet enough people to make enemies.'

'If he's been in an accident or been taken ill, you'll certainly hear soon.' Honey paused. 'We're here discussing two young dogs that were also on the shoot and that seem to have been stolen.'

Daniel's eyebrows, which were as red as the rest of his hair, almost disappeared into his ginger thatch. 'You're surely not suggesting that my father had anything to do with that?'

'One person and two dogs disappearing immediately after being present at the same shoot may be a coincidence,' said Honey. 'But coincidences always cause us coppers to sit up and sniff the air. Right, Allan?'

'That's right, Inspector,' said PC Webber.

Having made her point, Honey's voice slipped back into conversational tone. 'Tell me, does your father really like dogs?'

Daniel smiled sadly. 'That's the one point on which not one of us resembles him. I think he rejoices in the knowledge that a dog won't argue with him but agrees with him, right or wrong. Our dislike of dogs goes back to when we were very young and Dad kept an Airedale terrier that would give you a nip as soon as look at you. I think, looking back, that the dog was jealous and we didn't know better than to demand attention from Dad all the time. We were all terrified of Basker –

that was its name – but Dad couldn't see past the brute. To this day we all dislike and fear dogs whereas he can't pass a dog without a pat and an ear-pull.' He sighed. 'It's sad, really. I'd like to like dogs. Most of them have nice natures. I just can't bring myself to trust them whereas Dad can make any dog into his friend in a few seconds.' He focused on Honey and frowned. 'But you can't possibly imagine that he'd fall for a couple of spaniels and disappear with them. There's no way to make sense of it.'

'At this stage, I'm only trying to gather what facts I can find. I'll try to make sense of them later. Most of them will turn out to be irrelevant.' Honey tried not to sound peevish but this was the tedious part of her life story. By the very nature of investigation, the public were often asked questions that would prove to be quite irrelevant – in hindsight. 'If there's neither sight nor sound of him by this evening, you should report his absence. If he is then deemed to be a missing person, the machinery will go to work. I'll put in a report so that whoever's given the case doesn't have to start all over again. Leave your family's names, addresses, phone numbers, fax and email addresses with me and then I think you might go and try the hotels, like you said. You'll probably find that he's holed up with some lady.'

'I understand. But I doubt it. He isn't the sort to pick up a companion.'

Honey was about to ask whether suddenly meeting a lady out of his past might not have led to a romantic interlude, but Jackie had never switched off the computer. 'You have email,' it announced in a bland, female voice. Jackie jerked to life. She keyed up two messages. 'Just acknowledgements,' she said drearily.

'I'll run along and try the hotels,' Daniel said. 'Thank you. You've been very helpful. I hope circumstances don't force us to meet again.'

That evening, Honey wrote to Poppy ...

and as you can imagine the two young lovers are absolutely devastated. I've helped them all I can, but at the moment we have no real starting point. We may get a lucky break, of course, or the messages that I had them circulate may bear fruit – if I'm not mixing my metaphors unduly – but otherwise it seems pretty hopeless. Two spaniels have vanished, with only their microchips to identify them. Unless they come to the attention of somebody with a microchip reader, that could be the end of the story. The avail-

ability of a bolt-cutter suggests that this was no kind of teenage mischief.

Your ex has invested a lot of emotional capital in those dogs. (Was it Kipling who wrote about giving your heart to a dog to tear?) Fortunately the girl, though she was understandably knocked sideways at first, is emotionally sturdy and the two have almost total mutual absorption, so she may carry him through, for a while at least. But I suspect that this has taken first pressure on that hair-trigger of his. I have warned him not to go off half-cocked. I could imagine some well-meaning stranger arriving at the door, meaning to return two wandering spaniels, and being thoroughly duffed up.

So. We must just hope for the best but fear the worst. If you were thinking of sending a message of hope and sympathy, address it to both of them. Regards, Honeypot.

Chapter Seven

DI 'Honey' Laird arrived at work on the Monday morning determined to find some excuse to turn her attention to the missing dogs. She went early to the dog unit in order to clear that particular desk first, but she found a message awaiting her – a message that was duplicated in her share of the office in the main building. Detective Superintendent Blackhouse required her presence as soon as possible.

It was soon made clear, and not for the first time, that his interpretation of the words *as soon as possible* differed radically from hers. She was subjected to what seemed like an endless wait in the uninspiring corridor-cum-waiting room outside his office while other officers were allowed into the presence to report on current cases or to be assigned new ones. To pass the time, she was given a file to read, but this, in addition to her own two reports on the dogs and Henry Colebrook, emailed from home the previous evening, contained only a brief note to the effect that Mr Colebrook was now officially a missing person.

When admitted at last, she found Mr Blackhouse transmogrifying from his usual state of angry contempt into the image that she liked even less – the benevolent patron. Sometimes she thought that he was trying to grab the credit for having invented her. He did not go quite to the length of rising to greet a female subordinate but he made a token shift of his considerable weight as if for two pins, if these were well placed, he might have done so. When on first acquaintance he had vented his contempt on her, she had accepted this as part and parcel with his slumped posture, excessive weight, off-the-peg suits and general reputation. When she had wrong-footed him by her success with two cases that he had pronounced insoluble, he might well have been confirmed in one of his famous spites; but she had made no complaint when he took all and rather more than the due credit for the successful outcomes and with a breathtaking change of attitude he had decided that she was both brilliant and beautiful (in which he may not have been so very wide of the mark) and also in need of his protection and patronage, which assumption missed the mark by a mile. At least his benevolence had not yet extended to sexual approach and because Mrs Blackhouse was known to be a tigerish and possessive lady it seemed unlikely that it ever would.

When his heavily jowled face with its pocked and flattened nose was contorted into what he presumably believed to be an amiable expression, he said, 'You seem to have had a busy weekend. I have your two reports here. You think the two events are connected?'

'It's rather early for drawing conclusions, sir,' she said. 'He's said to have a soft spot for dogs, but one can hardly see him falling unexpectedly for a particular couple of spaniels, setting out to steal them the same night and disappearing with them. And yet, that's the only way that one could imagine a link.'

In the early days of their relationship he would have pounced on what they both considered to be a piece of sloppy thinking, but he chose to approve. 'Well reasoned,' he said. 'But the two cases are also connected geographically. You were in both places and you're our only senior dog expert. I want you to take them both on. Hand the dog unit over temporarily to the sergeant.' (She heaved a silent sigh. The sergeant was a newly promoted handler. She would be lucky to resume control of the dog unit and find that the paperwork was fit for anything but lighting fires.) 'Come to me for resources, but to start with you'd better take Sergeant Bryant. He can pick out a constable. Let me know who and what you need as you build your team. That's to say, if man and dogs don't turn up soon. Keep me posted.'

Detective Sergeant Bryant looked every inch a married man – clean and tidy, unimaginatively dressed, with very shiny shoes, tending towards overweight. He had a thin moustache. Honey had seen him around and thought him one of the better-looking men apart from the moustache. Unfortunately, he was of the same opinion but without any prejudice against thin moustaches. His looks were ruined for the moment by a swollen and brilliantly red tip to his nose. The effect was comical. She had to struggle to keep a straight face and the effort showed.

His thin lips showed signs of pursing. 'I had an insect bite,' he explained. 'I've been given an antibiotic but it may take a day or two to kick in. There's no way I can keep a dressing on it and still breathe.' He was making an overt plea for sympathy.

She decided to be helpful in the hope of starting off with a good relationship. In theory, there was no rule that they like each other, only that they work well in harness without actually fighting, but the best teams were usually harmonious. 'When we get down to my car, I may be able to help you. We'll need a constable, probably a whole lot more if this drags on, but one constable to start with.' She tried not to look at him, but even in the corner of her eye the ruby red of his nose still seemed to glare with the inevitability of a traffic signal. She was afraid to ask his first name in case it turned out to be Rudolph. 'Two of my dog handlers are down to one dog apiece, pending new arrivals, and I thought I might detach one of them. That way we get an intelligent helper and a general purpose German shepherd.'

Bryant turned to look out of the window, sparing them both embarrassment. 'I thought your dog – Pippa, is it? – was supposed to be a good tracker. That's what they say.'

She felt a momentary flush of pleasure, that her amateur dog was being accorded professional status. 'Pippa can be very good on her day but only at tracking. She's not fully trained and, being young still, she's easily distracted. For what it's worth, you can read this file while I use the phone.'

She asked Control to find out where Constable Picton was. The answer came back that he was training his dog at the Royal Observatory. She sent a message that he was to meet her at *Thack an Raip*.

She carried the file with her. At her car, she looked in the glove-box and found a small stick of 'concealer' – flesh-coloured foundation makeup. She left him to make use of it while she let Pippa out for a comfort break. It was always in her mind that she would have hated to be confined with a bursting bladder. When she returned, he looked almost normal. The swelling would go down in its own time, but with the colour hidden he was no worse than slightly odd-looking.

With the concealment of the hideous red tip to his nose, he seemed to recover an overconfidence that had been in abeyance. 'Shall I drive?' he enquired.

It is not unusual for a sergeant to chauffeur his superior, but he made the offer in a tone that managed to suggest that she should hand over to him, the male, for reasons of safety and time. She rarely allowed any but her most trusted acquaintances to drive her precious Range Rover, but she managed to ignore that piece of male impertinence. Instead, she demonstrated her own ability by slicing through the traffic without resorting to klaxon or flashing light. She could sense his feet pressing imaginary brakes and could almost feel his toes curling. She knew that she was only confirming him in his worst prejudices but she felt obliged to press on.

Picton, in one of the small dog-unit vans, had an encyclopaedic knowledge of the smaller roads around Edinburgh. He also had a shorter distance to cover from the open ground at Blackford and was already waiting at *Thack an Raip*. He was a tubby, grey-haired man in brown overalls – unflattering but well suited to not showing dog hairs. She gave him the file to read while she spoke to DS Bryant. He could hardly do much damage in a mile or two, she thought. 'Take my car,' she said. 'Drive – carefully – over the hill and find Moonside House. See the housekeeper, Margaret McLaghan. Get what you can from her and beg something of Mr Colebrook's to give the dogs a scent. Picton and I will join you shortly. Pippa will be all right with you.'

She cringed as DS Bryant set off. The car had an automatic gearbox, which limited his scope for wheelspin, but he set off fast, keeping his foot hard down and hammering over the potholes. She let him see in the mirror that she was watching him, but without persuading him to slow down. Perhaps she should not have shown off the car's paces.

Jackie was waiting in the doorway. They exchanged negative signals as she came to meet them. Her usually cheerful face was becoming haggard. She said, 'For God's sake try to keep it upbeat. He's very down. He's imagining them being sold to a Chinese restaurant or something awful like that.'

'We'll do our best,' Honey said. 'This is Ewan Picton. He's from the dog unit, so I thought that he'd be the best person to tell us if we've covered all the options.'

'Come inside,' Jackie said. 'I'll show you. We've had no real replies yet, only acknowledgements.'

'Give it time.'

Andrew was sitting, staring at a blank TV screen. He was hardly recognisable as the quiet but contented man that Honey had become used to. His face too was haggard – even in distress, he and Jackie seemed to react identically to emotions – and he seemed to have shrunk. The scar from his head wound, which was not usually notice- able except as a shadow at his temple, now shone pink. Honey sat beside him and attempted cheering words. Jackie stood behind him and massaged his neck.

Jackie had kept methodical notes of all emails and phone-calls. Picton looked through the list. 'That seems complete,' he said, 'except that we might inform the dog units of other forces. Folk walk dogs and dog handlers get to know them. I'll fix it as soon as I get back to the office.'

'One of us will come back later,' Honey told Jackie. 'If anything turns up, you have my mobile number. We'll come straight away if you call.'

They fitted themselves into the van, property of the dog unit. Picton's German shepherd, Dancer, was lean and dark but he had all the handsomeness for which Alsatians are note- worthy. He regarded Honey curiously through the mesh screen.

Picton drove up the farm track, which was in better shape than some. The potholes were scarce so that it was easy for a careful driver to avoid them. At the crest of the low hill they arrived at the farm buildings belonging to Jackie's father, all bright with paint. The substantial farmhouse was set behind the barns. Mud was remarkable for its scarcity and even the smell of dung was barely noticeable. Honey noticed that the field gates were in good order, provided with proper latches and with rope or wire not in evidence. This, she had always felt, was the test of a good farmer. The track continued between fields, but its condition worsened and the van bounced over ruts and potholes. Honey began to long for the comfort of her Range Rover. The track twisted through a narrow plantation. There was another secondary road ahead and another substantial house, almost the twin of the first. The name Moonside was displayed in raised, white lettering on an oak board at the gate. Honey's Range Rover, apparently undamaged, was parked beside a nearly new Mini. Beyond the road, the cluster of farm buildings seemed to have been extended and in some way modernised.

DS Bryant came out to meet them, brandishing a sock. Honey made sure of taking her car keys off him and said, 'Give it to Picton. Ewan, you and Dancer go round the place with particular attention to where a car may have been parked. We want to know whether Mr Colebrook, the wearer of the sock, has been here within the last twenty-four hours.'

'Yes, Ma'am.' This was said with a covert glance at the Detective Sergeant. In the privacy of the dog unit he would not have been so formal.

'You may as well take Pippa with you. You've worked with her in training.'

She opened the back of the Range Rover, called Pippa out and told her to sit. But Pippa was distracted by the presence of her old friend Dancer and slow to obey. Honey repeated the command.

'Sit,' Bryant said sternly.

Honey ignored him but, having finished exchanging courtesies with Dancer, Pippa sat anyway. DS Bryant exuded satisfaction. Honey fumed. Every dog lover resents that common irritant – the stranger who gives their dog an order, apparently under the impression that their own authority is greater than the owner's. But there was no time for revenge just then.

Bryant led her into the house. Margaret McLaghan ('Maggie', she insisted) was waiting in a bright kitchen. At least two dogs could be heard, scrabbling curiously at the door from a back passage. There was already fresh tea on the table in a fine china pot with matching cups and saucers set out. Ms McLaghan was a well-rounded lady of between forty and fifty-five. Honey would not have cared to make a closer guess as the housekeeper's hair had been dyed an improbable red, perhaps in an attempt to colour-coordinate with her employer, and she had applied her makeup from a strong palette and with a heavy hand. Her figure, however, appeared to be nearly all her own and was plump verging on good. Her accent, stemming from one of the genteel or lace curtain parts of Edinburgh, was too refayned to be credible. Her bow, when she was introduced to Detective Inspector Laird, could have been considered either polite or condescending.

There was the inevitable delay while tea was poured and biscuits dispensed. Honey knew only too well that any attempt at serious discussion during that process would be subject to recurrent interruptions. The sergeant had produced his notebook and was obviously eager to open the proceedings, but Honey said, 'Let Ms McLaghan tell it in her own words. Then you can fill in any gaps.'

'It's Mrs McLaghan. Or Maggie, which-ever you like,' the housekeeper said.

'Maggie, then. Let's have the story. When did you last see Mr Colebrook?' She had asked variations on that question a hundred times before but she still had an urge to refer to 'your father'.

Maggie needed only a fraction of a second for thought. Her memory had been re-freshed by answering the sergeant's ques-tions. 'Frayday nayte. Ay gave him his dinner at six, just as he layked. He preferred to go to bed on an empty stomach. He told me that he had an early start in the morning, so not to get up for him but to leave out the makings for his breakfast. He never takes more than cereal and a slayce of wholegrain bread with real butter of a morning.'

'And you went to bed, what time?'

'Ay was late. Well, if Ay was going to have a long lay in the morn there was no hurry. After Ay washed up, Ay walked his dogs and then watched the telly in may room until late, not far off midnayt. Then Ay went to may bed and slept until nearly nayne. Ay expected him back on Saturday nayt, but when there was no sign of him and no phone-call about dinner Ay took it that he was going to be late again. Ay was concerned, Ay don't mind telling you, because whenever he decaydes to dayne out he's very relayable about letting me know. Ay had a pair of lamb chops ready for him, but Ay ate them mayself. Yesterday morning, Ay found that his bed had not been slept in.'

'When you saw him on Friday evening, he was his normal self? Not depressed or worried about anything?'

'He was just as usual.'

'Are any of his clothes missing?'

'No, Inspector. Ay have looked. As far as Ay can see, he is away with what he stood up in, his shooting breeks and a tweed jacket, green stockings, warm underwear, leather boots, shirt, tie and his coat and hat. Nothing else, not even a toothbrush.'

'And if he had met a lady...?'

'You can put that thought out of your maynd, Inspector. Ay have known Mr Colebrook for upwards of ten years and he is past that sort of thing.'

It was Honey's opinion that no man was ever so far past 'that sort of thing' that the sleeping monster could not be woken again. She wondered whether Maggie's certainty might not derive from the fact that she was already providing for Mr Colebrook's needs, but she was saved from commenting by the entry of Ewan Picton. He had circled the house and outbuildings with Dancer and Pippa. The only recent scent of Mr Colebrook was where it was to be expected, between the front door of the house, the adjacent garage and the place on the gravel where he usually parked his Audi.

Honey set the two men to a scan of Mr Colebrook's papers and a preliminary search of the house while she continued to interrogate Maggie McLaghan under the guise of a girl-to-girl chat. Mr Colebrook had sold his supermarkets and had invested the money with care, mostly in a spread of annuities. He took the *Financial Times* regularly and seemed pleased with what it told him more often or not. All accounts were settled promptly. A starting assumption therefore was that there could be no shortage of money.

Unless his sons were a drain on his resources? But no. Mrs McLaghan was firm on the point. Mr Colebrook, when the sale of his own businesses was completed, had made a substantial gift to each of his sons and his sons had then set up their own business in the agricultural buildings across the road. On occasions he had let down his hair in speaking with the housekeeper. The business belonged to the sons, this was quite clear, but the father still owned the buildings, was a director of the company and was always available for help and advice although he seldom if ever visited the premises. He made it clear that he wished his sons to stand on their own feet. That was the limit of her knowledge.

The sergeant and the constable were still busily engaged. She left her mobile with them, asked the sergeant to join her as soon as he reached a suitable point for breaking off and then walked across the road. On closer inspection, the agricultural buildings were cleaner and tidier than the usual and the front had been given a major facelift. A sign that had not been visible from the farm track stated simply that this was the home of Colebrook Products, adding telephone and fax numbers and an Internet address. Several cars, none of them cheap, were parked outside the entrance and three vans had gathered at an open loading bay. There was no visitors' entrance as such but a door close to the loading bays bore an inconspicuous sign that read 'Reception.' Evidently casual visits by the public were not to be welcomed.

The interior more than lived up to the

outside. The buildings had been lined and they were air-conditioned to a point of perfect comfort, but they were streamlined and functional rather than welcoming. There were no windows, only universal fluorescent lighting. She crossed a shining floor and knocked on a glass partition behind which three ladies were marking copy invoices. One, a dusky blonde with a slight twitch, came to the sliding hatch. They embarked on another conversation of which Honey had endured a dozen duplicates in the past. She asked for Mr Colebrook Junior. Which one? Which one was in? Mr Leo was in at the moment. Then she would see Mr Leo. What was it about? Resisting the temptation to say 'None of your damn business,' she produced her warrant card. Evidently word of the disappearance of Mr Colebrook *père* had reached the business. Within a minute she was ushered into an office so sleek and modern that it hardly seemed to belong in a converted barn at all.

Leo Colebrook got up to shake hands. He was slightly younger than his brother and he bore less resemblance to their father. His hair was sandy rather than red and his nose lacked the Roman bridge. His expression was wary.

'I met your father at the Tinnisbeck Castle shoot on Saturday,' she said.

'So you're the young lady,' he began. His voice was pitched a little higher than those of his father and his older brother. He paused, embarrassed, and began again. 'I had never met the Carpenters, so of course I wasn't invited. Dad stopped on the way home and phoned me from the car. We talked business for a minute – nothing of the least importance, I assure you – and he said how much he'd enjoyed his day out, what a good company they'd been and he was rather complimentary about a young lady – a member of the police, he was given to understand – who he said was not only an excellent shot and a good dog-handler.' He stopped. The remark seemed incomplete. *Not only*, she thought, was usually followed by *also*. But also what?

But this was mere curiosity and female vanity. She moved on. 'Did he say how far along the road he was when he phoned?'

Leo frowned while he tried to remember. 'No,' he said, 'or if he did it didn't register with me.'

'What time was that?'

'I couldn't be sure. I had somebody with me at the time and my mind wasn't on it.

The staff were showing impatience, so it might have been around five-thirty.'

'Well, what did he say?'

Leo hesitated, seeming slightly disconcerted. 'Only to confirm that he'd enjoyed himself, like I said. And he asked me to let him have a spare set of accounts because he'd been working on them while under a misapprehension about something we'd already agreed and his copies were all scribbled over. I told him to chuck his copies away and I'd have a clean set ready for him.'

'Tell me what you know of your father's history.'

Leo looked into the distance, beyond the solid walls. 'I think he's fifty-eight. He was born in Surrey. He inherited two corner shops in the south of England when he was young and he spent his working life building up his little empire. He was very successful. He had the knack of management and of handling staff. I must say that I learned a lot just from watching him. He always planned to retire at around fifty and that's exactly what he did. He had always been fond of Scotland – our mother came from hereabouts – and he arrived at a deal with Mr Fulson, who wanted to enlarge his land. Mr Fulson took over the land and Dad acquired the house and farm buildings. He sold up and helped us, his three sons, to set up a business of our own where we reckoned there was a huge gap in the market. I'm the one who takes after him in business management, so I run things here. Vernon, my elder brother, is the country lover. He shoots and fishes so he does the buying. He can talk to keepers, farm managers and game dealers in their own language. Daniel's the sociable one, very hail-fellow-well-met, so he's the salesman. He's always out and about, lunching with hotel and supermarket managers. He should be as fat as a pig but he never seems to put on an ounce. And he and Harriet do a lot of entertaining, not my cup of tea at all – that's another way I take after Dad, in liking a quiet life. But we're all interchangeable and we muck in together. The arrangement works very well and there's rarely any friction.'

'And what exactly do you do as a business?'

'Didn't I say? And, of course, the signboard doesn't tell you much. We're on the game.' Leo laughed although the joke seemed to have been worn threadbare. 'You know that eighty per cent – that's four-fifths – of the pheasants shot in this country and sold to the game dealer for pennies go abroad, still at stupid prices? Those that remain on the market locally turn up in the butcher's shop, still in the feather, at a fiver or so. The British housewife has never learned to think of the pheasant as food although it's tastier and cleaner than chicken and it's been treated more humanely – well, if you were a chick, would you rather be fattened and then killed as soon as you were of edible size, or turned out into the wild to grow on and take your chance over the guns, with a better than fifty-fifty chance of surviving? We buy up some of that surplus and reckon to get it into the shops, oven-ready, for well under a fiver a *brace*. It's catching on.'

'I bet.' Honey was interested in spite of herself. 'What do you do for the rest of the year?'

'Venison. Meat, pies and sausages.'

'I *thought* something was ringing a bell. You're Colebros, right?'

'Absolutely right. Would you like to see the plant?'

'Very much. Your venison pies are good. I'd like to see where they come from.'

They were interrupted before the tour could begin. DS Bryant arrived, was admitted and handed Honey a note. She scanned it and said to Leo, 'Your father's car has been found, parked outside the Bell-bridge Hotel. As far as is known, he hadn't been inside, they don't remember serving him a meal and there are no signs of him.'

Leo got to his feet. 'I'd better go.'

Honey sat where she was. 'You'd be wasting time and petrol,' she said. 'His car is, or will be, in the hands of the laboratory technicians. I don't want to upset you, but you can see for yourself that they'll be looking for signs of foul play or illness or accident or intent to commit suicide or take flight. I'm advised that two detectives have been sent to make enquiries locally, to find out whether the car was seen arriving there. There's nothing useful you could do and you wouldn't be allowed near the car anyway. You'll be notified when you can collect it.'

'Of course.' Leo sank back into his chair and lowered his head. 'I should have rea-lised. It gets worse and worse.'

She decided to be brisk. 'I don't see it that way. You were short of your father and of a nearly new top-of-the-range Audi. Now we've recovered the car and we know a little more about your father's movements. That isn't all that you wanted but it can't all be bad. Perhaps you could leave it to your office staff to let your brothers know. Then we could do that tour. Sergeant Bryant might be interested.'

After a moment of thought, Leo agreed.

The buildings stretched further than Honey had imagined, all meticulously organised. There were storage rooms for newly delivered birds or beasts. In one large room, pheasants were being put through the whirling rubber fingers of a plucking machine. Dressing, cleaning and packaging followed and the processing lines finished at the cold stores. Damaged birds were diverted to where three large ovens prepared the game and venison pies, stews and other products. Cold stores ensured that goods could be delivered, frozen or fresh, to the customers. Honey was relieved. She had recognised several products that she had used and that June continued to buy; but all was clean and hygienic. Tiles and stainless steel dominated the scene and there were wash basins and notices about hygiene at every corner.

The only person to remain unimpressed was the sergeant. To him, in common with many urban dwellers, *pheasant* was a dirty, or at least a foreign, word. As they left the plucking room he said, 'I suppose you pay the girls extra for working in there.'

'In point of fact,' Leo said, 'they queue up for a place there. They're given gloves but they never use them. Working every day with their hands coated in pheasant grease, their hands become beautifully soft. Their husbands and boyfriends appreciate it. Have a look at a book of old wives' medicines some time. You'll be surprised how many of them feature goose grease.'

The feather particles floating on the plucking room air had induced in the sergeant an enormous sneeze, in coping with which his handkerchief had removed the concealing makeup. His nose was again shining like a beacon, to the amusement of the staff, but Honey was becoming tired of his manner and pretended not to notice. The sergeant took the smiles that greeted him at every doorway as being of admiration or friendship and responded to each with a condescending wave. The continuous background noise prevented him from hearing the giggles that followed on behind.

Chapter Eight

Although she did not know it, Detective Inspector Honoria Laird was approaching the most frustrating days of her police service. As it became ever clearer that Henry Colebrook was not going to reappear, her small team grew by the addition of another detective constable and a retired sergeant to collate the probably negative information that kept rolling in. They pried into the lives and movements of the missing man, his sons and business contacts. Telephone accounts were demanded and eventually received. In desperation, Honey requested authority for DNA tests to be made of the debris vacuumed from the missing man's car and from the clothes in his cupboards, but the investigation was still only a missing person enquiry and in view of the high cost of each individual test her request was turned down.

Their enquiries embraced also the missing spaniels and included the assumption that the two cases might be connected, though no member of the team ever came up with a plausible theory as to the connection.

If all that effort produced any gems of information, they were unable to detect them. Most cases give the investigating officers some point of departure – a trail, however faint, to be followed until it becomes a roadway or a glimpse by a witness to form the basis of a public appeal or a door to door enquiry. But this investigation was producing only a picture of perfect universal respectability. This had to be an illusion because people *en masse* are seldom models of virtue. They have peccadilloes, large or small. But nothing relevant came near the surface.

The result was a gradually increasing air of despondency. Detectives may sometimes wait years for the breakthrough in a murder case; but this was a case in which there might not be a victim and, if there was indeed a victim, he had utterly vanished without leaving a clue behind. People do occasionally vanish into the hardcore beneath motorways, but these are usually men at whose departures the police may heave a sigh of relief. But Henry Colebrook, so far as they could discern, was a taxpayer and a respectable citizen. On the other hand, there was always the haunting possibility that Mr Colebrook had departed of his own volition, as he was perfectly entitled to do, and that the spaniels had been liberated out of malice by some of the local tearaways and were running free. The possibility that Mr Colebrook had stolen them and then decamped in accordance with some previous plan began to emerge from the lists of improbable explanations and to assume more and more an almost imperceptible gloss of probability.

She emailed to Poppy:

Spot and Honey seem to have vanished totally. Neither they nor their microchips have surfaced. We have, we think, been in touch with every canine organisation in Britain if not the civilised world, but without the least whisper of a helpful reply. For the moment one can only hope that they are alive and well treated.

In the circs, it is sad but not surprising that your ex is taking it very badly. He was not notable for his stability before this fell on him; only Jackie and the spaniels held him on a level keel. Now he broods. He is convincing himself that his worst fear, that they have been disposed of by some Asian restaurant to their diners, is the truth. It is a measure of his humanity that he agonises over what the dogs, if alive, may be thinking; and it is useless to tell him that dogs do not think coherently, as do some but by no means all humans, he knows different. He seems to be heading for a breakdown or worse. Not drinking or drugging, praise be, but the most massive case of clinical depression that I ever saw. His doctor gave him an antidepressant, but that only switched off his sex-urge – which was not a cure for depression and was soon abandoned!

It is not for me to make suggestions, but a complete change would help. Could you bring yourself to invite him along with his ladylove (fiancée, did I tell you?) for a visit? Some sunshine and a warm sea, and meeting your dogs again, might ease the waiting period His first reaction would be to remain on the spot but I think I can convince him that there is nothing that he can do locally and that he could be back here in 24 hours if we get a break. I would promise to keep them informed regularly.

Her inevitable restlessness was aggravated when Sandy, whose fraud case had turned out to be tangled with a similar series of frauds under investigation by Scotland Yard, was required to visit London regularly and for days at a time. As a minor consolation, Sandy's absence did at least make it less of a wrench for Honey, with Pippa in tow, to visit her friends the Carpenters at Tinnisbeck Castle, for a couple of days 'or as long as it takes', in order to squeeze the last drops of information out of that area while Sergeant Bryant, supervised over the telephone, continued the fruitless round closer to home.

The first day she spent in the company of Ian Argyll. The other Ian, Inspector Ian Fellowes of Newton Lauder, had put his own small team to local enquiries, but it could not be assumed that Mr Colebrook had vanished on their patch so that the case did not properly belong to them. Thus there was no depth to their reports. Honey went over much of the ground again with Ian Argyll, but there could be no doubt that as far as his own friends, relatives and contacts were concerned, he had done a more thorough job. Each was vouched for by others and nobody had acquired new spaniels. Pat Kerr, who had been introduced to the shoot by George Brightside (the keeper), was known to keep a Labrador-cross-collie and Ian had established that, according to the lady next door, no other breed of dog had been over his threshold in many months.

While pursuing that topic, Ian Argyll had also set his extended family to enquiring after Mr Colebrook himself. Most of them had met the quiet older man on the day of the shoot without either liking or disliking him; but nobody had seen or heard anything of him since he drove off from the castle shortly after the shoot had broken up. She went over much of the ground again, but Ian had been thorough. A walk about the back lanes of Tynebrook village produced no suggestion of unaccustomed dogs and Pippa showed total indifference.

That left Hannah Phillipson and Johnny Cruikshank – he who Jackie had thought 'rather nice'. Armed with detailed directions from Jeremy Carpenter, she set off on the second morning, following the unimportant road that passed the castle and threaded the village.

The Scottish Borders include two low-lying and fertile coastal plains, east and west, but between the two the land is wild, still much as it was when the Border Reevers were wont to emerge and pillage. Honey followed the road as it wound gently between hills that were sometimes grassy and sometimes heather-covered. After ten miles in a generally westerly direction she took to a by-road, single-track with passing places, signposted to some speck on the map of which she had never heard. Sheep looked up from the sparse grass to watch the car. The tarmac finished suddenly after a mile. The unpaved road went on but a short driveway led into the smallholding occupied by Ms Phillipson and her partner.

The house looked well built but it was evidently in need of paint and several new windowsills. One slate was down in a gutter. The place had a sad look, as of a lack of money or of anybody to care. She parked where there was gravel, at the side of the house. The back door had a long, dark, wet-looking streak where the paint had opened.

As she turned back into the car to take out her shoulder-bag she heard the latch click behind her. To her surprise she was not confronted by Hannah Phillipson nor by her 'fluffy and clinging' housemate but by Johnny Cruikshank. If she had been told that he was a frequenter of the smallholding she had forgotten it. She must have let her surprise show. He smiled suddenly, re-deeming his unremarkable face. 'Were you looking for the girls?' he asked. His voice was rough and touched with the Borders accent.

The boundaries between *girl* and *woman* and *lady* are hazy and may depend on the age or attitude of the person making the choice, but Honey was of the opinion that Hannah Phillipson at least was past the age for being thought of as a girl. On the other hand, the term implied a degree of intimacy. If Cruikshank was the lover of either or both of the women, the flattery might be forgiven.

'I was.'

'They went to the shops. They'll be back soon, if they haven't met somebody to talk to. Somebody said that you're a police inspector.' His accent was neutral and his turns of phrase suggested that he was not uneducated.

'They were correct.'

He paused and then nodded. 'Let's not stand around in the cold. I was just going to make coffee.'

Coffee, she thought, was exactly what she most needed to chase away the chill of the day, but a chance to poke around while the ladies were absent was too good to miss. 'I'll walk my dog for a minute and then come and join you,' she said. He nodded and turned back into the house.

Honey fetched Pippa out of the car and gave her a sniff of Henry Colebrook's sock (carefully preserved in polythene) but kept her on the lead. The smallholding was set in a pocket of fertile land among the hills. They circled the house between beds that were tidy but showing vacant strips where vegetables had been lifted for the table. The apple trees were now bare. They had been pruned with some skill. Several large clamps could have held one or more bodies but were more likely to hold turnips or potatoes. A hoe leaned against a clothes-pole. Honey inverted it and pushed the handle deep into each clamp, but Pippa sniffed without interest. Generous timber outbuildings held well-kept tools including a rotavator and a miniature tractor, a supply of sheep nuts and some well-ventilated shelving laden with carefully separated cooking apples. In one small shed a rough table had been given a top of stainless steel, presumably for butchering the occasional sheep or lamb. The same small room had been flyproofed and two rabbits, six woodpigeon and five pheasants were hanging. She could safely assume that the pheasants came from the Saturday's shoot and that Cruikshank's brace had been pooled with the rest. Honey nodded to herself. In the cold weather and in the unheated shed, the pheasants would need hanging for at least another week to tenderise them. How much longer for the sake of flavour would depend on the taste of the diners. Two large chest freezers of commercial pattern stood ready to accept the products. There was nothing in the least out of the ordinary for a rural smallholding.

In a larger shed against the boundary she found signs of cottage industry in the forms of a half finished tapestry and a solid old treadle sewing machine. A skirt in process of hemming lay beside the sewing machine and in a rack against the end wall were stored some folded lengths of various cloths. Garments hung on hangers nearby. That, she thought, even supplemented by the produce of the two or three acres of land, would hardly support a menage of three or even two people, but of course there might be some other resources among them.

In the faint hope that Henry Colebrook might have sought sanctuary there, instead of shutting Pippa into the car she brought her into the house with her. In the farmhouse style kitchen they found Johnny Cruikshank along with a collie/Labrador cross that she remembered seeing at work on the day of the shoot. She had thought at the time that there was a strong resemblance between the dogs of Johnny Cruikshank and Pat Kerr; some careless owner had been presented with an unplanned litter. Pippa and the other dog exchanged suspicious sniffs and each decided that the other was neither threat nor rival. They lay down amicably enough near the warmth of the range.

Cruikshank, meanwhile, held a chair for her before pouring what turned out to be unusually good coffee. He was in his later twenties, a nice-looking man who might have been handsome in a bony, Highland way if his teeth had been straightened. As he put the cups down, she became aware that he was eyeing her in a manner far from platonic – in fact, she began for the first time to see some sense in the old cliché about a man undressing a woman with his eyes. With her own background in unarmed combat and with the ladies of the house due to return shortly, she felt perfectly safe. It was not even unpleasant to be regarded with desire provided only that the desire was respectful. Nevertheless, she inched her chair forward so that her legs were hidden and inaccessible under the table.

He stood behind her for a second. He was probably enjoying the silhouette of her breasts against her silk blouse, but she decided not to make a fuss. On the other hand, this individual could benefit from a little bullying. Jackie had thought him 'rather nice', but perhaps she was responding to some elemental sex appeal that was hidden from Honey. She took out her notebook, slapped it open on the table and produced a pen. 'Your full name?'

He pulled up a chair and sat down across from her. 'John Wesley Cruikshank.'

'Your address?' She held his eyes.

'I live here,' he said with a touch of defiance.

'How long have you lived here?'

'Two years now.

'Occupation?'

This time he really did flush. 'I do the work about the place, attend the sheep and do the vegetables. What's this about?'

'You don't know?'

'Of course I don't know.' He began to bluster. 'How could I know? What are you suggesting?'

'Did you hear about dogs and a person disappearing after Saturday's shoot?'

There was a silence. She had time to look around the room. Typically old-fashioned and rural. She rather liked the polished clutter – well equipped, everything to hand and yet not unhygienic. Copper utensils, probably too good to use, adorned the wall, blue and white china filled the shelves.

126

'Yes, of course I did,' he said suddenly.

'It took you a long time to work out that I'd have to know you knew. What with bobbies from Newton Lauder asking questions and Ian Argyll doing the same. So why did you ask what it's about? What else did you expect the police to visit you about?'

'Nothing.'

'Come on. Policemen had been round asking questions about what happened at a place and time when you were present and you have to ask why I'm here?'

'No,' he protested loudly. 'I was distracted.'

'By what?'

'By you.'

Obviously she had not slapped him down hard enough. That line of questioning could only lead onto dangerous ground. 'Then pull yourself together and look elsewhere, and we'll get down to what I came for. What did you think of the pair of springers that Jackie Fulson and Andrew Gray were working?'

She was watching him surreptitiously while he considered, but there was no sharp reaction. 'They were pretty good,' he said.

'Did anybody in particular take a fancy to them?'

He was relaxing. 'Everybody admired

127

them, but that's not the same thing, is it? The only one I saw making a fuss of them was the old man, the one who you're looking for. Mr Colebrook. Very taken, he was. When he gave them a peppermint, they'd offer him a paw to shake and he loved that. But I don't think he really cared that much about dogs and anyway he wasn't the sort to pinch them. His style would more have been to pull out a fat roll of twenties. If the roll was fat enough, they'd give in.' He sat up suddenly and brightened. 'Then, when they heard that he'd vanished, they started the fuss about the dogs being stolen in the hope they could get the dogs back and still keep the money.'

Well, it was a new theory but not a very credible one. It hardly accorded with her impression of Andrew and Jackie, who anyway had surely not known of the disappearance when they first demanded her help. 'How did you get on with Mr Colebrook?' she asked.

He shrugged. 'Hardly exchanged a word. See, he was one of the Guns and I was only a beater.'

She decided to make a guess. 'You were talking together at lunchtime.'

'Well, yes. But only to say he was shooting

well. It was the truth.'

'I agree. But you walked up the track with him to the first drive after lunch.'

'I was walking behind him, not *with* him.'

'What was your impression of him?'

He scratched his chin while he thought hard about the question. 'He's a nob, a gent – he shook hands with every beater at the end of the day. He was friendly, but he's a chancer. I didn't mind that. I'm a bit of a chancer myself.'

This was a new slant. It takes one to know one. 'How do you make that out?' she asked.

'It's just impressions. But... One thing. He walks like an old man–'

'He *is* an old man,' she said.

'All right, you tell it.'

'Don't be saucy with me or I'll start checking the details of your life.'

'No need to get steamed up,' he said quickly. 'You wouldn't find much wrong with my life. Yes, he's an old man. Well, not to say old, but getting on a bit. He walked like an old man. But sometimes he'd get a fresh spring in his step as if his knees and hips had stopped bothering him. Of course, that does happen. Arthritis comes and goes between rest and exercise; and a good dram of malt makes a good anaesthetic. But by my reckoning he put on the limp a bit whenever he wanted sympathy or to be spared a lot of walking. And it worked. Whenever the beating line came up with the guns there he was, in the place nearest to the vehicles, and I don't remember him walking as a flank Gun ever.'

Thinking back she thought that he might be right, but that that was probably due more to the consideration of Jeremy or whoever was mustering the guests at that moment. Before she could say so an interruption became imminent. There was the staccato rattle of a well-worn diesel engine and a boxy Land Rover was turning in at the gate.

'Have you any more impressions or observations about Mr Colebrook?' she asked quickly. She could hear two women's voices exclaiming at the presence of the Range Rover.

He hesitated. If he had uttered the thought in his mind both cases might have been solved there and then. But he decided that it was an irrelevancy and not worth wasting the time of the police. He said, 'No.'

'You'll call me if anything comes back to you?'

'Yes, of course.'

The door opened, admitting a gust of cold air followed by the two women. Hannah Phillipson's companion was, as she had already been described, a fluffy blonde. Her hair, Honey thought, was genuinely fair. Her face did not quite live up to it, being thin and with a rather pointed nose. Her figure, however, was excellent. Honey had been blessed with the sort of slenderness that many women only dream of and a metabolism that retained it with only a modest restraint on her appetite, but she had occasionally considered that she might have preferred a slightly chubby voluptuousness such as she now recognised. Men, she had found, liked to look at the supermodel's figure but they recognised instinctively which would be the more comfortable to grasp. Oh well, she told herself, Sandy seemed satisfied. Hannah introduced her companion as Gemma Kendal.

In the field and surrounded by men, Hannah had seemed to have her share of femininity; in the context of her home she seemed to have grown and toughened and her jaw took on a definitely masculine slant. It would have been quite possible to visualise the two women as a pair of lesbian lovers but

Honey immediately sensed that that would be an unduly facile assumption. She had come across several lesbian couples in the course of her work. The sudden arrival of an attractive, well-dressed and evidently well-heeled young woman had usually set emanations of suspicion and jealousy filling the air while each partner worked out whether the other was attracted and, if attracted, likely to do anything about it. On this occasion the signs of jealousy were there but they were not directed against Honey. The looks darted at her were not unfriendly but a coldness was evident between the two women. They addressed each other in tones of great politeness. Johnny Cruikshank, on the other hand, was thanked several times for the provision of coffee and there were solicitous enquiries as to whether he was over-tiring himself.

That told her all that she needed to know about the household. This was no pair of Sapphic lovers but a *ménage à trois* with all the concomitant undercurrents. She guessed that the two friends had set up house together but that the arrival of a man had set up stresses and strains in the three-cornered relationship. Honey wondered whether she could exploit them to garner extra admissions but no opening sprang immediately to mind. For a moment she wondered whether a little flirtatious behaviour towards him might not provoke some revelations but decided to save it for another occasion. Instead, she identified herself to Gemma, explained her mission and asked for a private interview with Hannah Phillipson. The other two left the room – Johnny Cruikshank, she thought, with some relief.

Hannah helped herself from the coffeepot and took the opposite chair. 'I'll help if I can,' she said.

Honey jotted down the basic details. (Hannah's middle name was Jane.) 'What did you think of Henry Colebrook?' she asked.

'What should I think? He pinched my bum during the lunch break,' Hannah said. 'What do you think of a man his age who goes around doing that?'

'When a man gets past the age for sex, the drive often comes out in other ways,' Honey said tolerantly.

'But he isn't past the age. That's my point.'

'How would you know a thing like that?'

Hannah looked offended. 'I just know. Look, I have a very keen sense of smell.' (Honey looked. The other certainly had not been hiding when noses were handed out.)

'I can smell the male smell of a man and, if he's clean every other way, I can tell when sex dies on him. I don't know why, but I can. I must be smelling testosterone or pheromones or something. And if he fancies me it gets stronger.' She smiled wryly. 'That doesn't happen very often but it happens.'

That, if true, reopened the possibility that Mr Colebrook had eloped. She jotted a note to remind herself to check on whether any ladies in the general area had vanished or gone away. She also decided to try a day without even her usual faint trace of perfume and find out whether her sense of smell was equally informative. Or had Hannah's imagination been running away with her? 'Very interesting,' she commented. 'We shall have to call on you when we get an old man involved in a sex abuse case,' she said. 'Anything else?'

Hannah frowned. 'Not that I can think of. He stood next to me at the buffet table or I'd hardly have known him.'

'What did you think of the two spaniels?'

The frown became an instant smile. 'Brilliant little dogs. They were a joy to watch. It's always a pleasure to see something done well. And such pretty manners!'

'Did you see Mr Colebrook with them?'

'Yes. They seemed ill at ease with him at first but when he started slipping them bits of cocktail sausage they soon took to him.'

Honey laughed. 'Typical! Since then, you haven't seen or heard anything of Mr Colebrook or the spaniels? And you'll phone me if you do?'

'Of course I will,' Hannah said sincerely. It seemed that under her mannish exterior was a soft heart. 'I hate to think of that nice young couple, waiting. They doted on those dogs, and the dogs on them.'

'Do you remember anything that Mr Colebrook said during the day?'

'The only thing I remember him saying was that it was turning into a fine day. And when I said that he was shooting well, he thanked me and said that he was managing better now that his longstanding fibrositis was improving. Is that all for now?'

'Unless you can suggest anything else I ought to ask you. No? That's it, then.'

All three came to the car with her. Her impression was that Cruikshank came in the hope that he might manage a little flirtation and the two ladies came along to make sure that he didn't. In the event, the ladies were distracted by the arrival of the butcher's van. Cruikshank took his chance to lean into the Range Rover and say, 'You have a good-looking leg there.'

She looked at him coldly. 'I have two of them,' was the first thing that came into her mind so she said it.

She saw amusement deep in his eyes. 'Aye, you have,' he said. 'And between them I don't know where to look.' He turned away. She was sure that his shoulders were shaking. She drove back to Tynebrook village turning the remark over and over in her mind. Did he really know what he was saying? On the whole, she thought that he did.

Chapter Nine

Hannah Phillipson had offered her lunch at the smallholding, to take potluck with the unusual household. Honey was tempted to accept in the hope that some casual word, uttered in the pique of the moment, would furnish the connection that she was sure was to be found somewhere. (Had she but known it she had already been offered the clue that she wanted, if only she had noticed.) But the tensions evident between the trio would have made for an uncomfortable meal, the offer had been made grudgingly and she was expected back for lunch at the castle. She had a deep-rooted dislike of mind changing.

Lunch at the castle turned out to be a hasty meal because the Carpenters, with many apologies, were hurrying into Edinburgh to meet a relative. Honey set off again. Although George Brightside, the keeper, had broken with tradition and, at Jeremy's invitation, had been shooting with the Guns on the Saturday afternoon, she had barely had a dozen words with him. She called at his home only to be told by his wife that he would undoubtedly be with 'those dratted birds'. She drove the short distance between the village and the castle yet again. She kept a pair of miniature Zeiss binoculars in the glove compartment and a scan through these produced no sign of the keeper on the grouse moor. She nursed the Range Rover over the rocks and potholes of the track, over the crest to the broken ground, a landscape of boulders, gorse and coarse grass, where she found the keeper topping up his feeders and water drinkers. His Labrador, as worn with years as himself, watched his comings and goings with placid eyes. The pheasants, which a week earlier would have clustered around his feet, had now learned that life was real and earnest and there was a price to be paid. They had withdrawn to the fringe of the bushes, still waiting expectantly but ready to explode into noisy flight if startled.

On the shoot he had given her the impression of being a benign old soul, but that may have been the result of being free at last to take a pace back and join in the harvest for which all the effort had been made. Expectation of substantial tips may have helped. While at work, he showed a more irascible side of his nature until he realised that Honey, who had dressed in a well-cut denim jacket and skirt sturdy enough to withstand a day in the country, was quite prepared to help carry bags of wheat or buckets of water. She saw him glance at her waistline, wondering whether her pregnancy was advanced to the point where carrying would endanger the foetus. Evidently he decided that it was not, or else that it was unimportant. The pleasure of stretching her muscles doing work on a fine day in beautiful country took her back to earlier days in Perthshire, but she went carefully all the same, assessing the effect of each load on her musculature before accepting it. She was carrying in her womb the future president of the world and she had no intention of endangering him – or her.

George Brightside waited until the work was done before seating himself on a straw bale and saying, 'Well, what's it about?'

Honey had no wish to carry away with her any more straw and dust than was inescapable. She brushed herself down, fetched her shooting stick from the Range Rover and seated herself facing the old man. It was comfortable in the sunshine. There was an illusion of intimacy. 'The two spaniels,' she said.

'Ah,' he said, nodding. 'I thought it would be that. Summun said you're a Bobby. But they've a'ready been at me about that, over and over.'

'So what did you tell them?'

'Good pair of dogs. One was the better hunter and the other the better retriever, but either could do both jobs. What else do you want to know? I saw the owners put both dogs into the back of the Land Rover and their pheasants on the back seat. Then they drove off. That's the last I saw of any of them.'

'Did anybody follow them away?'

He surprised her with a prompt answer. 'Miss Phillipson left next, but that was ten minutes after and she went in the opposite direction.'

'Did you notice anyone who was particularly taken with the dogs?'

He frowned and his nostrils flared. 'Mr Colebrook was giving them titbits, but he did that for several dogs. I checked him for that. People don't like their dogs made fat and the mistress didn't put up snacks for them to be given to the dogs. He said he'd only given them peppermints, but I told him that a dog isn't a guard dog if it thinks strangers bring food, see what I mean?

Honey saw exactly what he meant. In her experience, a dog expecting a biscuit could make a damned nuisance of itself. One of her phobias was being jumped up against and mauled by the muddy paws of somebody else's dog. 'What about Mr Colebrook?' she said.

'Never arrived home, did he? Ian was asking round about that. He took his two birds and drove off, polite as you like. Didn't have a dog but I'll say this for him, he tipped well. And he knew what he'd hit or missed. He picked up his own birds when they was close by and when they fell further off he knew exactly where they were.'

'Good for him!' she said. A few more questions failed to produce anything new about Mr Colebrook or the spaniels. 'Now tell me about Pat Kerr,' she said.

The keeper looked at her in surprise. 'Him? He was just a beater.'

She looked sharply at the old man. Was this an example of the snobbery of Guns versus beaters that, though it was unusual in the Borders, sometimes raised its head in the more upmarket shoots? 'How do you mean?'

'I didn't see much of him on shoot day. I was busy in the morning and among the

Guns in the afternoon.'

'But you brought him, so I'm told.'

George Brightside's brow acquired some additional wrinkles. 'I wouldn't say brought, exactly. See, he lives just outside the village. He spoke to me outside the pub one day. He said he was new around here and didn't have any contacts and could I do with his help now and again? I saw his problem. You've to live a long time around here before you're a local – a hundred years at least. Well, there's times I can do with casual help and I will say that he's a good worker and knows how things are done. But I wouldn't say that I ever got to know him. He's not a man that lets you get to know him easily, not unless you've got...' He moved his hands, miming a big bosom. 'Then, before the shoot, he asked could I use another beater? I was going to need all the beaters I could get and I hadn't seen or heard anything against the man. A beater gets to know the ground well, sometimes too well, but in a close little area like this I'd damn soon hear if he started poaching. So I said to join up with the other beaters outside the pub and I warned Mr Carpenter to expect him.'

'And he's proved as harmless and reliable

as you hoped?'

Brightside's wrinkles suddenly twitched and reappeared at right-angles. He seemed amused. 'He hasn't done me any harm.'

Honey was feeling her way but she thought that she could sense how the land lay. If they had been sitting any closer she would have poked the other in the ribs. 'But he's a bad boy. Is that what you're saying?'

'And he's not alone.' He glanced around as if to see that no eavesdroppers were lurking among the gorse. 'I may as well be the one to tell you this. See, one way or another I meet up with most of the folk around here and I hear most of the gossip. And I can put it together. I know where you were this morning, for instance. Your car was seen.'

She was quite used to the speed with which news travels among country folk. 'So?'

'Johnny Cruikshank. Nice looking lad, wouldn't you say?'

'I might. But he's another bad boy. Is that what you're saying?'

The old keeper was smirking. 'You'll have heard of the eternal triangle? Well, how about the eternal square?'

'You'd better explain.'

George Brightside was in no hurry to start working again. 'I'll tell you,' he said. 'When those two women moved into Tarn Croft, years ago now, everybody thought they was a couple of those – what d'you call 'em? – lesbians. You know what I mean?'

Honey laughed. 'You're asking a woman police officer if she's heard of lesbians?'

He chuckled. 'Then, about eighteen months or two years back, that Cruikshank moved in with the pair of them. That caused a stir, I don't mind telling you. Some still thought they was lesbians, but it was the others that had the right of it, because they're not too fussy about curtains, being at the back of beyond so to speak, and the postie saw more than he was meant to and he was definite. Cruikshank was keeping them both warm, alternate nights it looked like. Still is sometimes, I'm told. But then Pat Kerr arrived. What do you think happened?'

'Two couples?'

'You'd think so, but not a bit of it. Seems Cruikshank still pleasures the both of them. But the way it worked out Miss Kendal fell for Pat Kerr. He doesn't mind giving her a tumble now and again but he's set his sights on Miss Phillipson; and she still can't see past John Cruikshank while Johnny's all for Miss Kendal. How do you like that?' He chuckled.

144

'Not a lot,' Honey said. 'It can make a lot of bad blood. Jeremy would have had to keep the two men apart in the beating line, I suppose.'

'Bless you, no.' Brightside was evidently relishing what he was relating. 'The two men still get on fine. They meet for a drink several times a week. They don't talk openly about the goings-on. They keep the talk between themselves but when they've had a drink or two their voices get louder and, well, others can overhear. It's just a big game to them.'

She did not bother to exclaim at the callous attitude of the average predatory male. Though herself secure, she was well aware that sex may be a game, a battle of wits, to a man. In her bachelor days she had played the same game. 'It's a game that's likely to end in tears,' she said dryly.

'That could happen. Yes, it surely could. Anyway, I thought you should know. And now I must get around my traps.' Satisfied that he had stirred up a little trouble he pottered off, the picture of elderly benevolence.

Armed with detailed directions from the keeper, she set off to find Pat Kerr. She found his cottage half a mile south of the village. It was one of a pair and his neigh-

145

bour, a stout lady of Jamaican extraction, said that he drove a van for a living but was usually home 'about now'. This presumably was the lady who had stated that no dog other than Pat Kerr's own had been near the place. It was beyond Honey's power of imagination to visualise the Jamaican lady lying her head off for love of Pat Kerr. She walked Pippa once around the immaculate garden without observing any reaction except at the pigsty tucked neatly away in a corner. Then she waited, soothed by Rafael Puyana playing baroque pieces on the harpsichord via a CD in the Range Rover.

Ian Argyll, driving by in a large, new-looking van, spotted her. She gave him a wave. He pulled up and got out. She killed the music and invited him in beside her. He reported on a total lack of progress in the matter of the dogs.

'Keep listening,' Honey said. 'But I wanted to ask you about something else. It's probably nothing to do with anything much but I was set wondering. You know where I was this morning?'

'Tarn Croft?'

She smiled. 'Everybody knows everything around here, but you know even more than most. Tell me, what's the situation up there?

Somebody suggested that Miss Phillipson was sweet on John Cruikshank but that he fancied Miss Kendal who couldn't see him for Pat Kerr.'

The joiner hesitated but the gossip was too good to pass by. 'You'd think that that was the way of it,' he said slowly, 'but it's a dashed sight more complicated than that. You'll see either of the men with either of the women, and not just out for the shopping. Not unless they dress up all fancy to go into town for the supermarket. Miss Kendal in particular. She's as often out with the one as the other, but last time I saw her dolled up she was with Cruikshank. Gave me a real surprise, she did.'

'Being with John Cruikshank you mean?'

Her shook his head impatiently. 'I mean I thought Johnny'd got himself a new girl. She looked five years younger and a de'il of a lot prettier. I've no eye for a woman's clothes, but there's many a model would be glad to have that figure of hers. Well, her figure's much the same most days, it's her face and hair that changes. That evening, it was her face that had me baffled. I had to look and look to be sure that it was the same woman. Clever! Well, I may be a joiner to trade but I can get the whole job done. I've worked with painters a lot, clever fellows some of them, and I've learned about counter-shading and the like of that. I had a lad came to do one job for me and showed me how he could change the shape of a room by clever use of tones. Well, I got a damn good look at her across the bar and her face was still there under the shading. But she'd used her makeup so damn cleverly that you could have put her alongside one of those film stars and she'd still have looked good.' He turned in his seat and studied Honey critically. 'You've no need for that sort of trickery,' he said.

'Well, thank you,' she said.

'A pleasure,' he said. She thought that he was going to go further. The way gossip travelled out in the country, she would not have been surprised if he knew of Cruik-shank's one-liner about her legs. But he only nodded and got out of the car.

Kerr made his appearance a few minutes later. He drove what turned out to be a baker's van around the outlying farms and crofts. He had finished his round but he made her wait while he cashed up, cleaned out the van and fed a few leftover rolls to a brace of large pigs in the sty. The garden contained a small paved area with a teak seat

148

where he invited her to settle. There was even a solidly built table to take her notebook. The pigs must have been very well kept because their smell was barely discernible, so she accepted the suggestion that their interview be alfresco. The lady neighbour was indoors with all her windows closed.

When he joined her on the garden seat his dog, the spaniel-collie cross, settled at his feet. The dog was restless, scenting that Pippa had been over his territory. Honey had not noticed anything on shoot day but now she realised that Kerr had more than his fair share of sex appeal. His face had rough good looks and he seemed to be exuding testosterone as other men might distribute BO. In days gone by, Honey might well have fallen for his approaches. Even now, she felt a sudden desire to have Sandy home again. She was in no doubt that he was equally aware of her.

Kerr said, 'I suppose it's about Mr Colebrook. The mannie as went missing?' His voice was almost accentless.

She decided that she would dictate the pace of the interview and she would come to Mr Colebrook in her own good time. 'How long have you lived here?' she asked.

He looked surprised but not put out. 'About a year,' he said. 'Perhaps a bit over.'

'And what brought you here?'

There was a flicker of annoyance across his face. She thought for a moment that he was going to challenge her right to interrogate him. Then he relaxed. 'I was born not far from here. I grew up in the country. But there seemed to be no way for an ambitious young lad without capital to get on. I took to the building trade, worked in London through the boom years, as a brickie. Those were the good years. "We pay so much a thousand and you can work as many hours as you like." A man prepared to work his arse off could save some money in those days. I had a girl then, but she died.' He paused and then hurried on. 'In the end, I got fed up of city life. I'd made some money and it was time to let up, take it easier and enjoy life, so I had a friend send me the local rag. I was looking for somewhere like this, within my means.'

'And are you enjoying life?' she asked.

He hid a faint smile. Honey was not supposed to know about his amorous arrangements. 'It's worked out fine,' he said. 'I'm a vanman on weekdays, which gets me out and about and meeting people. Evenings or

150

weekends I help Dod Brightside if he needs it or I do odd jobs. I trained as a brickie but I can do most jobs around a building site. I don't break my back laying bricks at so much a thousand any more, except for Ian Argyll if he needs help, and I don't owe any man a damn thing. Is that what you wanted to know?'

'Some of it. Why did you ask to be taken on as a beater? Not for the money, surely?'

He looked at her sideways. 'What would you know of a beater's pay?'

She recognised a touch of left-wing inverted snobbery. 'Twenty quid if you're lucky. Or ten and a brace of birds. I've gone beating oftener than you have, I bet.' She did not mention that most of her beating had been on her father's estate.

He was suitably abashed. 'Well, I didn't know that, did I? No, it wasn't for the money. But the beating line's one place where the men gather who know most of what's going on in the countryside. Who's got what and who wants what, you follow me? And going round in the van, I have my ear to the ground. I can sniff out a deal. I already told old George I could get him wheat cheaper than he's been paying for it.'

So he was a wheeler-dealer. That brought

to her mind several questions that she could use to bring him to heel if he needed it.

'What did you think of the pair of spaniels?' she asked.

'Good pair of dogs.'

'What value would you put on them?'

'Depends who was selling them, the owner or a thief.'

'Say the owner.'

'Spayed? Microchipped?' He suggested a price that she knew to be not far wide of the mark.

'So who do you think might have taken them?'

He raised his hands in a negative gesture. 'Not worth anybody's while to do it for money. Anyone could guess that they'd be microchipped and probably tattooed as well. Too much risk altogether. My guess would be that somebody fell for them hard.' Unconsciously, his hand fell to toy with his dog's ear. 'Dogs are easier to love than people.'

She could have given him an argument but it would have been based on a single exception. Anyway, there was a lot in what he said. 'Now tell me about Mr Colebrook.'

He had begun to relax. Now she felt him tense. She felt it through the teak seat and saw the minute change in his posture. 'Pleasant old lad,' he said. 'Friendly.'

'Tell me about him.'

'What's to tell? I saw him on the shoot. We never spoke.'

'You'd met him before.'

He hesitated. She knew that she had startled him although he had himself well in hand. 'Why do you think that?'

'I saw you look at him and I recognised recognition. When somebody answers a question with a question,' she said, 'I know they're trying – unsuccessfully – to hide something. While you were down south, laying bricks at so much a thousand, you were technically self-employed. Did you ever make a tax return? And did you draw benefit?'

'No!' he said loudly.

'No you didn't make a tax return?'

'You got me muddled. Look, what do you want to know?'

'I want to know what you know about Henry Colebrook. Everything.'

'I don't know that much,' he said plaintively. 'I just didn't want to let on that I'd ever known him in case you thought things.'

'What things?'

He managed a sort of smile. 'The sort of

things you're thinking now. It was a long time ago, after I went south. I did a job for Mr Colebrook at one of his shops, that was all. I thought I recognised him and when somebody said his name I was sure. He didn't want to let on that he knew me, so I didn't bother. Satisfied?'

'What do you think happened to him?'

'How the hell would I know?' he demanded irritably. 'But if I was forced, really forced, to make a guess I'd say that he wouldn't be the first man to make a fool of himself over a woman. Or a dog.'

Chapter Ten

Home, for Honey and her husband, was a well-built, medium-sized house dating from the tail end of the nineteenth century. There was no possibility of a garage, but most of the front garden had been laid with tarmac. The remainder was bright, in summer, with flowers in tubs and baskets. The Lairds had spent good money to bring the kitchen and bathrooms well up to date and had themselves worked hard on the decoration. Honey was a dab hand at papering and, because she could bend low more easily than Sandy, her services were also called on for the painting of skirtings.

It was a good house in one of the pleasant small streets just off a main thoroughfare, and Honey was usually happy there. Now, however, it was one of Sandy's periods for being called to London and the house was empty except for June, who was no real company and had interests of her own. June had been brought up on the periphery of an affluent household where her mother, being the housekeeper, had taught her not to be familiar with her employers. Honey spent the Wednesday and Thursday catching up with the fruitless efforts of her small team, writing reports and dragging the admin of the dog unit back on the proper track. Two of her earlier cases were approaching court and the depute advocate general was asking all the questions that he should have asked months earlier. The weather had broken and a slow-moving depression was said to be dropping rain, usually heavy, on much of Scotland and parts of England and Wales. (Her impression was that it was always raining in Ireland anyway.) She was therefore not displeased to be kept occupied in the warmth and comfort of indoors. She took work home with her in the evenings.

On the Thursday evening she emailed Poppy.

Your invitation reached your ex and his new love. They are thinking about it. Oddly enough, it is Andrew who is dragging his heels. Jackie might well have hesitated at taking her fiancé on a visit to his ex-wife, but either she trusts him totally or she is so besotted with him that she would give him up to you if she thought that you could make him happy – which, of course, you couldn't. Andrew himself is listless. As I feared, he feels that he should be at home in case the dogs make a miraculous reappearance, but he has reached a state of depression in which he will go wherever he's dragged. I still think that he'd be better away from here and from all the reminders of happier times. When I saw them today, I played on the fact that Jackie had never seen the south of France. I think that you'd better set your staff to airing the best guest bed.

On the Friday morning she was studying a copy of Mr Colebrook's will. It took an unusual form. Because much of Mr Colebrook's fortune had been gifted to his sons, he had invested most of the remainder in annuities, which would die with him. There were bequests of personal property to the sons. The residual legatee was the housekeeper. This provision caused Honey to set the team searching for some unseen asset but not even a winning lottery ticket was to be found.

She was interrupted by a summons to the presence of Detective Superintendent Blackhouse. She expected strictures about her failure to find the dogs or the missing Mr Colebrook, but Mr Blackhouse was pleased to be understanding. After enquiring about her health and the continued success of her pregnancy, he came down to business. 'You seem to have covered all the possibilities,' he said. He leaned back in his chair and prepared to pontificate. 'Either the dogs will turn up or they won't. The same applies to Henry Colebrook. But people usually appear. If they went of their own accord, they come back the same way; if they're dead, human bodies nearly always surface. You can dispose of a dog's corpse without the law taking much interest, but human bodies are different. One glimpse of a human bone and everybody starts running around in circles. While you wait for that to happen, you can have a look at this.' He sat up straight and passed across a very thin file. 'Initially, the case belongs to your friend Fellowes in Newton Lauder, but it has a strong Edinburgh connection. Liaise with him. And keep me posted. The legal establishment's getting hot under its fancy collar.'

She had almost reached the door when he spoke again. 'One more thing,' he said. He sounded hesitant, almost shy. 'Somebody suggested that you would be looking for a godfather when your baby's born. Or maybe two. I just thought I'd let you know that if you don't have a queue of relatives lining up for the honour ... if you like ... if it would be of any help ... well, I'm available.' He humphed and became very busy with some papers on his desk.

Honey muttered something about being honoured and made her escape, resisting the urge to turn and bang her head on the outside of the door. Who in hell had made a suggestion so unwelcome, so inappropriate, so altogether infuriating? She would find out and eviscerate him. Or her, of course.

Back at her desk, it took another minute before she had stopped seething and was ready to look at the file. Immediately she saw why the legal establishment was getting hot under its collar. The only paper in the file was a terse and factual report, timed only an hour earlier.

Julian Blakelove QC was a very senior advocate indeed and was believed to be next in line when a judgeship became available. It seemed that on the previous evening he had given a lift to a lady whose car had broken down in the rain not far from Newton Lauder. His main residence, Hollington House, was nearby and so he had offered the lady shelter until somebody could come and get her car going again. According to Mr Blakelove, they were hardly inside the door when he was set upon. This seemed unlikely in view of the fact that his housekeeper, who was slightly deaf and slept in a separate wing, had found him in the morning, tied securely to a chair, stark naked. His wife's jewellery and two valuable paintings had been taken. There was no sign of the lady.

At first glance it seemed to Honey that her liaison would probably be limited to ensuring that none of the Edinburgh fences would touch the goods with a barge pole. She picked up the phone. Newton Lauder advised her that Inspector Fellowes was out at the moment. She was offered his mobile number but she already knew it by heart.

When she raised him on his mobile, he sounded delighted. 'Honey!' he said. 'Can you come through straight away?'

She looked out of the window at the rain still streaming down. 'Is there anything I can do on the ground that I can't do better from here?'

'There certainly is. The victim is being much less than frank but he did say at one point that he might open up to a woman officer; and I don't have one of those available except for a youngster who was directing traffic not long ago. Come direct to Hollington House. Bring Pippa.'

Honey sometimes suspected that her assistance was only requested because she usually brought Pippa along with her. 'Why do you want Pippa?' she asked.

'I don't know. But she always seems to contribute something.'

She called at home. Pippa seemed relieved at the prospect of activity and change as opposed to merely being walked. Their road lay over the Lammermuirs again, where a brisk wind was hurling rain against the car. Even the heavy bodywork of the Range Rover could do little to damp out the shrapnel rattle of the rain.

Between bouts of corrective steering she managed to muse. Rumour had it that Julian Blakelove was a bit of a goat. She knew that he was an exceptionally expensive advocate, habitually obtaining acquittals for kingpins of crime on the slenderest of legal technicalities, but from her occasional glances at the gossip columns she knew that he had also married money. His wife's jewellery was said to form an exceptionally valuable collection. The house and his *pied à terre* near the Edinburgh law courts contained, or had contained, much other evidence of wealth. Hollington House had therefore been equipped with all the latest security gadgetry connected by a secure line to the police emergency number. Mrs Blakelove was in the South of France, visiting relatives. And if Honey could gather that much information without even trying, a dedicated criminal could search out much more.

Hollington House lay half a mile along a side-road leading to nowhere of the least importance. With it went several thousand acres of second-rate farmland but prime shooting territory. (She knew that her father and Julian Blakelove had at one time exchanged shooting invitations but no friendship had developed and contact had not persisted.) The house itself was a modestly commodious one of perhaps eight or ten bedrooms and a small servants' wing, built about a hundred years earlier to accommodate some minor landowner and his family and guests. The gardens were small but well kept, melting into the surrounding woodland and the moors round about. The house was severely Scottish in manner but a *porte-cochère* in matching style had been included. This was already occupied by a car that she recognised as belonging to DI Ian Fellowes, but there was just enough space to allow her to squeeze the Range Rover under cover and to get out and ring the doorbell without suffering more than a few drops of blown rain.

Ian Fellowes himself came to the door and admitted her to a large hall decorated with more extravagance than taste. The only smell present was of the most expensive polishes. For once Ian seemed to be less than his usual cheery self. He even omitted his customary greetings. 'I'll just introduce you to the victim,' he said, 'and then I'll go and join PC Bright, who's trying to squeeze a little extra out of the housekeeper and her husband, the chauffeur-gardener and man-servant. I don't hold out much hope. He's as deaf as a post and she's terrified of putting her foot in it with her boss. She untied him, by the way, instead of cutting the ropes, so we'll learn nothing from the knots. That, I suppose, was her thrifty Scottish soul rebelling at wasting a perfectly good clothes-line. He'll talk to you, but alone.'

'Have we any idea why?'

'I'd be guessing. You'll soon know. Probably.' He led her along a lushly carpeted hallway and opened a heavy door. 'Detective Inspector Laird. From Edinburgh,' he added. He hurried away in the general direction of the servants' quarters. From his tone and an almost inaudible hiss at the end of the introduction, she guessed that he had been quite unable to decide between protocol and prejudice and had eventually failed to arrive at a decision as to whether or not to add a 'sir'.

The room was handsomely panelled in oak. A vast but uncluttered desk, racks of books and comfortable chairs suggested that the room was a masculine study where he could feel secure and superior. Julian Blakelove QC was established in a large chair of buttoned leather. She had seen him in court. Now both the chair and his quilted dressing gown seemed slightly too large for him, which went along with her impression that he had shrunk slightly. He had always been slightly pop-eyed but now his eyes were also watery, which she put down to lack of sleep. His manner, however, remained larger than life. He did not bother to rise. 'Come in, young woman,' he said. 'Come in and let's have a look at you.'

She recalled that his manner in court was as hectoring as a judge would let him away with, but even in his own home she was not going to let him get away with sexist arrogance. She crossed the floor and took a seat on a more upright chair, dug out her notebook and looked at him. He was distinctly corpulent. His face was flushed.

'My appearance is irrelevant,' she said. 'Tell me, why did you insist on a woman officer?'

'Quite right,' he said gruffly. She guessed that he was covering a high degree of embarrassment by resuming authority. But embarrassment at what? 'Let's get down to business. Woman officer? I think you'll see as we go along. But put that book away. This is off the record except insofar as I agree.'

'You realise that you may be making a successful prosecution impossible.'

'Young lady, please don't try to tell me the legal implications of my own words. I will talk to you because without the detailed knowledge of the *modus operandi* your success would be even less likely. But I want certain parts of the story confidential and if that hampers your investigation so be it. I'll argue the point with the Lord Advocate if I have to. Do I have your assurance that what I tell you is off the record and remains known to you alone until I say so?'

In a few seconds of frantic thought she saw possible hazards ahead. 'Provided that I get a letter to that effect from you. After all, you could drop dead or change your mind

165

and I could be left in the position of having suppressed evidence.'

He looked at her, more pop-eyed than ever, and then gave a single bark of laughter. 'You're no fool,' he said. He heaved himself to his feet, moved to the desk and scribbled a few lines on headed paper, finishing with an elaborate signature. 'Will this do?' He dropped the page into her lap and settled back in his original chair without awaiting her reply.

She read it quickly, folded it and dropped it into her bag. 'I won't deliberately spill your secret, but you understand that in the process of preparing a case it may not be possible to limit the facts to your fellow advocates. Now,' she said, 'suppose you tell me the story in detail.'

'I had a client consultation yesterday evening,' he said. His voice, always noted for its mellow resonance, was recovering its tone. 'I left the solicitor's office about nine-thirty. It was such a foul night that I was tempted to stay in the flat I keep in the Grassmarket, but I had a lot of reading to do in the morning – this morning – and I decided to do it in comfort and without having to make my own breakfast, so I set off for home. If I was followed, I was quite unaware of it, but the whole thing must have been brilliantly timed and organised. When I got to the junction with the main road, there was a sports car stuck at the side of the road. The electrics were completely out and the electric hardtop had jammed in the open position.

'The bonnet was up and a woman was poking about at the engine. She was wearing a thin plastic mac over her cocktail dress but she looked pretty well soaked. She had folded a carrier bag to make a sort of hat, to protect her hair and make-up. She said that she had phoned for help but that other cars were stranded and the rescue vehicle might be another couple of hours. And to answer your next question before you ask it, no, I don't know the make or model of the car and I didn't notice the registration. I think the car was black or dark blue, that's all.

'It's a rather desolate part of the road and that car was going to be no shelter for her, so I invited her to come into my car. Well, no gentleman could do less. Eh?' He seemed to be asking for approval and understanding but Honey remained noncommittal. 'I said that I could provide her with a hot bath, a change of clothes and a comfortable place to wait. She quite agreed and said how thankful she was to be rescued. I spread newspapers to protect the leather and she got into the front passenger seat beside me. I noticed that she was wearing evening gloves, which I found rather alluring at the time, more fool me! Your forensic team has been and gone without finding a single fingerprint except mine, my wife's, my housekeeper's, her husband's and those of the lady who comes in to help with the cleaning. But I'm jumping ahead of the story.

'She removed the carrier-bag headgear. She was not particularly beautiful although her hair and make-up were skilfully done. I didn't notice anything remarkable about her face. Her hair was fair and I think that the colour was genuine with only a very little assistance. She had large, brown eyes and her make-up made the most of them. Her figure was extremely good. We arrived here and I opened the front door, of course keying in the code to switch off all the alarms. That much I told your colleague and that's about as far as the official version goes. From this point on, it's off the record except when I say so.

'As soon as we were inside she stood over the radiator and began to struggle out of the wet nylon mackintosh. But you know how those things can cling. She asked me to help her and I did so. You may believe this or not, just as you wish, but I swear that I was being a perfect gentleman. Then she started on her dress, which was thin and clinging and almost as wet and had to come up over her head. It also was clinging to her. She seemed very hesitant though I suppose she was playing a part. She never suggested being left in privacy. "You'll have to help me again," she said. I doubt if you could find one man in a hundred who could resist that sort of invitation.'

Honey rather hoped that Sandy would be that one man but she was not inclined to put him to the test. 'And is that why you wanted a woman officer? You thought that a woman would be less shocked by a little sex?'

His already florid face turned a duskier red. 'Good God no! I'll admit that I didn't want a lot of male officers sniggering together and passing the story around, but from what I've heard women are just as addicted to smutty gossip. I thought that a woman detective might get some sort of a lead from what comes next.

'I helped her, just as she asked. And, believe me, she was all kitted out in the very classiest, top-of-the-range, most alluring underwear that you could imagine. It wasn't wet; if it clung it was for a different reason. This was definitely not the cheap-and-tarty kind nor minimalist bikini things, nor even the high quality but modest sort, but real quality in every respect. I try to see that my wife has the best, but this was much better than I've been able to find in Edinburgh. Cream silk with a tiny patterned texture depicting flowers woven in, and so fine that I swear you could have read a newspaper through it. Lace that definitely came from Brussels. And the whole ensemble matching and superbly designed, not only to conceal but at the same time to provoke. It was one of a kind. Am I making myself clear?'

'Perfectly.' There could be no doubt that the lady had left home with every intention of leading some man into dalliance and Honey knew exactly what symbols of femininity could be guaranteed to rouse the devil in the man of a certain age.

'How long was the dress?'

'Below the knee.'

'Stockings and suspenders, I presume?' He nodded, looking away. That confirmed that the woman had definitely been expecting sex and probably with Mr Blakelove.

'Could you draw the designs?' she asked. 'Or describe them clearly?'

'Hopeless,' he said. 'Quite hopeless. I didn't notice the designs, just the effect.'

If the woman who had functioned as the bait in the trap had shopped for lingerie somewhere very special, it might furnish a link. 'Excuse me for a moment.' She went out into the hall and used her mobile phone. She gave instructions to Control for a car. June answered her next call immediately. There was a book that Honey had bought soon after leaving finishing school, when she had seemed to be on the threshold of a modelling career and before her father had put his foot very firmly down. She told June where to find the book, to wrap it in paper and to hand it over to the driver of a car who would be at the door within minutes.

She returned to the QC and resumed her seat. 'Finish the story,' she said. 'You had sex.'

'Why are you so sure–?'

'The way your housekeeper found you. Naked.'

'Oh yes.' He had some of the shamed look of a scolded dog yet at the same time she thought that he was savouring a memory.

171

He swallowed, secretly salivating. With an effort he drew himself up and recaptured some shreds of his dignity. 'You'll understand that by that time my – ah – passions were inflamed. My wife has been abroad for several weeks and this woman was in fact the summit, the very pinnacle of femininity. You know what I mean?'

Honey, who had in her time aspired on occasions to that same peak, said that she knew what he meant.

'I had no thought left about locking the door or resetting the alarms. I may say that she was more than willing.'

'And where did this transport of delight take place? You escorted the lady upstairs?'

'There's a big couch in the hall. You must have seen it.'

She had difficulty keeping the laughter out of her voice. The embarrassment of this usually domineering figure was so total. She was tempted to ask whether the couch was in the hall for use when his passions were too inflamed to allow of any delay, but she refrained. 'Go on,' she said severely.

'That's really all. I was only aware that an intruder had followed us in when the muzzle of a shotgun dug into my ribs. The man was in dark clothes and he had a dark ski-mask on, so I can only tell you that he was about average in height and not overweight. He seemed fit. He had trainers on his feet.'

'I suppose you didn't happen to notice the shotgun?'

This time he proved to have been more observant. She supposed that his attention might well have been focused on the gun. 'A rather commonplace side-by-side boxlock, twelve-bore,' he said. 'Possibly a copy of the AYA. Varnished stock with a semi-pistol grip. Well worn – much of the blueing had been rubbed away in front of the fore-end – but it looked as though it had been cared for.'

'Did he hold it as though he was accustomed to holding that particular gun?'

He frowned portentously as he struggled for recall. 'I don't have a lot to go on but I would say yes.'

'Go on, then. What happened next?'

'Next?' He was visibly relaxing now that they were back onto subjects of masculine awareness. 'There was hardly any next. They made me sit in the hall chair. He had brought in a new coil of sash cord and they tied me up, tightly, and taped my mouth. He had also brought in a carrier bag with dry clothes for her, but commonplace, nothing distinctive. They took the carrier bag away with them, but it was green and I think it came from Marks and Spencer. They left me there all night. It was bloody cold after the heating went off, I can tell you. It will be a miracle if I haven't caught a chill or pneumonia.'

Honey was not particularly interested in the QC's future health. She took the best part of a minute for thought. 'I'm going to bring my dog in,' she said at last. 'You can help me to lead her to wherever your two visitors stood or sat. I want her to get the scent of them both. Then there's a good chance that she'll let me know if we meet up with either of them in the course of our enquiries. It's one of her tricks.'

'Very well.'

She fetched Pippa. Ian Fellowes's car had vanished. The rain was going off. According to Mr Blakelove, the visitors had traversed no more than a small part of the hall, a large and elegant drawing room where the two pictures had hung and the safe in the study. Mr Blakelove opened the garage and his car for her and Pippa sniffed the seat where the woman had sat and the newspapers that had been put down to save the leather. Pippa

174

showed a stirring of interest, limited to the areas pointed out by Mr Blakelove, but that might have been because one of the visitors had trodden in something that was, by her standards, edible.

'They got the safe keys out of your pocket?'

'Exactly.'

She was returning Pippa to the Range Rover when a police Jaguar swept into the drive and made a circle on the sweep of gravel. A uniformed constable delivered a heavy parcel, neatly wrapped in brown paper. She found Julian Blakelove QC back in his deep chair and on the point of falling asleep. He awoke and regarded her with only slowly returning recognition.

She unwrapped the heavy book – *High fashion through the 20th Century – an Encyclopaedia – Volume 4.* 'I want you to look at the last chapter,' she said. 'See if anything rings a bell.'

He browsed through the beautifully drawn illustrations of lingerie, modelled by ladies only mistily portrayed. She had to recall his attention several times when his concentration seemed to wander, but at last he stabbed a page with a plump forefinger. 'That's it.'

The design identified was a set that she acknowledged to be one of the most exquisitely designed ever. She recalled from her modelling days, and was reminded by the text, that it had been designed to the order of a film company for a very special sequence. The film star Anne Munro had appeared thus clad in the film *Heat of the Night*. The sequence had only lasted for a little over thirty seconds, but the shot had figured prominently in the stills and posters. The combination of a beautiful young woman in beautiful lingerie had caught the public attention. Men had returned to the cinemas to see it again and the posters were now collectable items and commanding remarkable prices at auction.

Inevitably there had been offers to purchase the right to reproduce the designs, but the studio had refused to sell while the film was being shown and revived. Attempts to pirate the designs had attracted lawsuits, generating more valuable publicity, but the copies had never attained quite the jollity of the originals. As a result, the set had never been commercially produced. When the copyright reverted to the famous designer, she preferred to retain her rights and allow the design to be purchased, in the form of paper patterns, only by individuals for their personal fabrication.

'That will do for the moment,' she said. 'As to the lady, you've been almost lyrical about her figure and her underwear, but can you improve on your descriptions of her face and hair? Or did you not look at her face?'

He flushed and seemed about to make a furious retort. He reined himself in. 'I will let that insult go by. Yes, I looked at her face. Her hair was up and it was dressed in a French roll. Her face looked classically beautiful, but clever make-up had a lot to do with it. I know how deceptive you ladies can be.'

The QC was giving way to a series of enormous yawns. He could not have had much if any sleep. 'I'll leave you now,' she said. 'I suggest you go to bed. I'll be in touch.'

He was looking at her as though taking in her appearance for the first time, but his look was of puzzlement rather than lechery. 'Haven't I encountered you before?' he asked her.

'You have,' she said. 'But I can't blame you for not recognising me – it was several years ago and I was in uniform at the time. You cross-examined me in the Archibald Warren case. You suggested that I had taken a bribe from his victim's family to tamper with the evidence. I had to face an enquiry. I was cleared, but it can't have done my career any good. Warren got off and he killed again. Good morning.'

And that, she rather thought, would probably spoil his sleep for him. She very much hoped so.

Chapter Eleven

She was back in her office by mid-afternoon. She spoke first to Ian Fellowes. When she broke it to him that she had no intention of giving him the details of what she had learned from Julian Blakelove, Ian was loudly resentful. 'You can trust my discretion,' he said.

'Do you trust mine?' she asked.

'Of course I do.'

'Would you still trust my discretion if I gave away some details that I had been told in confidence and off the record?' She waited but there was silence on the line. 'I have a faintly possible lead,' she told him. 'I'll follow it up. If anything comes of it, you'll be the first to know. For the moment, I abide by my promise.'

'This is irregular.'

'It's not and you know it,' she said. 'It's normal to protect informants' information and identities. We may want his trust and cooperation in the future. If I don't keep my word this time, he won't trust us again.'

Ian sighed and they ended the call on a note of frustration.

Honey was in a fever of impatience. Friday was running out. Sandy was coming home for the full weekend and she was due to go off duty. The High Fashion Encyclopaedia had mentioned that the patterns were in the hands of the country's biggest postal retailers of dress patterns but the phone number quoted proved to be out of date. While the only available DC wrestled with directory enquiries, she rattled down a carefully edited report.

She got the retailers on the line at last, identified herself and asked for a list of customers for that particular set of patterns. The voice was not helpful. 'We do not give out that sort of information over the phone,' it said. 'There are matters of copyright and confidentiality.'

'There are also matters of police business.'

'You're only a voice on the phone to me. How do I know that you're a detective inspector?'

Honey had met this kind of Jobsworth in the past and she knew that trying to hurry it up would only cause it to think of more and more reasons to be obstructive. 'Phone me back,' she said. She gave the number. 'You'll find that you're speaking to Lothian and Borders Constabulary. Ask for Detective Inspector Laird.'

'Very well. If that checks out, I'll fax you the list. Is that the same number?'

She gave the fax number. 'When will I get it?'

'It'll be Monday now. The phone line will be open for orders for another few hours but the rest of the office is closing down.'

She bit back a vitriolic comment which would only have formed an excuse for more delay. She contented herself with making a horrible face at the ceiling, clenching her fists and saying the very rudest word that she could think of. She said it several times in succession. But she said it silently. She was alone in the shared office for the moment, but she still had to protect the bland and imperturbable face that she presented to the world.

Not even the tranquil state induced by a clear weekend with a loving and virile husband was proof against the frustrating times that were to follow. The promised fax only arrived, following three reminders, on the Thursday.

She had lost the services of Ewan Picton

for the moment because his dog, Dancer, rather than Picton himself was needed elsewhere. To her relief, Picton was replaced by a woman DC. Stella Weems was plain and dumpy but cheerful and efficient. Honey was able to delegate to her, in confidence, the seemingly endless task of tracking down, by telephone, the sixty-odd sets of paper patterns that had been sold. Several still languished in drawers, being considered too difficult to attempt until the purchaser had attained a higher standard. Some had been copied once or twice and then put away. Still others had been passed from hand to hand. And even such sets as had been made from the patterns might have been sold or given to a friend, relative or client. Seldom was there much indication as to what material or colour might have been used. The possibilities were endless, but somewhere among the jungle of names Julian Blakelove's seductress, or somebody connected to her, might be lurking.

A car answering the general description of the one used by the enticing lady had been stolen several months earlier. It was found, burnt out, near Kelso. Enquiries suggested that it had spent the intervening period in a lockup near Gorebridge, but not even the letting agent could give a reliable description of the driver. Enquiries revealed that it had several times been seen waiting in a lay-by on rainy evenings, but the top was always up and the occupant was apparently female but otherwise well concealed by the dark glass.

Detective Sergeant Bryant continued to be as irritating as a barley seed in an orifice and Honey soon concluded that he had been foisted on to her because nobody else would work with him. Even though she checked him, almost slapped him down, with increasing ferocity from time to time, his familiar and insufferably patronising manner always made a return. An uninformed bystander might well have thought that he was the more senior of the two. Yet he was an efficient if sometimes lazy investigating officer and somehow they managed to work in comparative peace, largely by dividing up the work and going their separate ways. Their efforts were unrewarded. Reports of young springer spaniels, singly or in pairs, had to be checked although none bore much resemblance to Spot or Honey. In the hope that the two dogs were still alive, she had all the emails repeated. Every report of a red-headed man in late middle age seen behaving in the least oddly had to be investigated despite the difficulties entailed in identifying an individual seen, usually days earlier, alone and in no particular context. Some of these were proved to be irrelevant; others remained unexplained, but of Henry Colebrook there was no sign. His credit cards remained un-used, his cheques unwritten. When she thought to ask the question, she learned that his brace of pheasants had still been on the back seat of his car but had soon dis-appeared, presumably into some policeman's freezer.

Every effort had been made to close off avenues through which Julian Blakelove's treasures, and more particularly those of Mrs Blakelove, might be fenced. They might be lying hidden until the heat was off; but equally there was no denying that the goods might well have gone abroad, quite possibly before the QC's housekeeper had so annoy-ingly untied him. Privately, Honey thought that both the investigation and the gentle-man's attitude might have benefited had he been left *in situ* until the scene and the knotwork had been studied by experts. It was possible, however, that he had been left in his bonds overnight in order to allow time for safe disposal.

The bank accounts of Mr Colebrook Senior were already available. In desperation she attempted to get access to the bank accounts of surviving personnel involved, but the bank managers were uncooperative and it was felt that there were no adequate grounds for seeking a court order. The mobile phone service providers were more helpful and soon she was wading through several massive lists of calls, some going back for many years. The collator, a civilian recently retired from CID, began to depend on her excellent memory, which made a change from the usually converse system.

This saga of endless marking time without progress continued for another two weeks. Then, on the Tuesday, Honey returned to her office at HQ, dispirited after an abortive trip to Helensburgh, a quick look at a spaniel she had never seen before and a tiring drive back in poor light and a thin, cold rain, to find several messages on her desk. A man's body had floated to the surface of a small loch near Galashiels. There was no identification yet but from first reports the body conformed roughly to the dimensions of Henry Colebrook and had greying red hair.

According to the note from Detective Superintendent Blackhouse, he intended to leave the investigation in the hands of Ian Fellowes in whose territory the body had been found, at least until the pathologist had reported and there was some indication as to how the man had died and whether he was the missing Mr Colebrook. DI Laird was to liaise and keep the DS informed. If it proved to be a case of murder he would take personal charge. An email from Ian requested the assistance of Honey and offered to provide accommodation.

Sandy Laird was away again so she had no objection to escaping from Edinburgh. She phoned Ian, who seemed to have recovered from his umbrage. He said that there would be no point in going to where the body had been found, and in darkness. The immediate area had already been trodden down and picked over. If she came straight to his house, there would be a meal.

No mention had been made of Pippa, but she knew that the Labrador would be welcome. Pippa had already been walked. Honey kept a bag packed ready for emergency departures and Pippa had a permanent bed in the tail of the Range Rover, so her call at home took only a few minutes. As she drove, her spirits rose. Dead bodies were never pleasant company and those that had been under water for any length of time were among the worst, but at least, if this should be the missing Mr Colebrook, the case would open up.

Wind and rain made driving conditions even worse and there were holdups caused by two accidents, but she pulled up outside Ian's modest house in Newton Lauder in two hours. Ian Fellowes hurried out, struggling with a golf umbrella, to help her in with her dog and small luggage to where Deborah was waiting with an enormous hug. The two women had become firm friends during Honey's first stay in the town, and the bond had been renewed during several subsequent visits.

Deborah could be very discreet, but when a case was local she preferred not to hear the details until it was over. During the meal they exchanged news and talked generalities. The Fellowes's young son had already been fed and when the meal was over Deborah took him off to his bed while Ian and Honey settled in the sitting room. The boy had been named Ronald and was known as Ronnie, after a disreputable great-uncle that Deborah had nevertheless dearly loved.

'One of Colebrook's sons,' Ian said, 'the

eldest one–'

'Vernon,' she said.

'Yes. He was quite prepared to make the identification. But it's about three weeks since his father did his vanishing act and, to be brutally frank, the body seems to have been in the water for most if not all of that time.' He looked at her as though wondering how delicate were her susceptibilities although he knew that she was no stranger to dead bodies. 'So I would not trust an identification made on facial appearance only. We're fetching his dentist up to the mortuary, here in Newton Lauder, first thing, before the post-mortem begins.'

'No help from the fingerprints?' she asked. 'Of course, I know what long immersion does to skin–'

'That isn't the problem. There are at least partial fingerprints left on the hands. Your Sergeant Bryant was helpful but he said that he couldn't furnish an authenticated set of Mr Colebrook's prints.'

'I'm afraid that he was right, for once,' Honey said. 'The trouble is that on the Friday, the day before the shoot, they had a carpet cleaning firm in. Next day, the housekeeper and her husband spent the day on a massive springclean, finishing with a polish and a wipe over all the surfaces. Even his keyboard and his brushes had been wiped. There are a few fingerprints in the house still, but prior to the big cleanup the sons and their families and God knows who else had been in and out of the house. We simply don't know which if any of the remaining prints pertain to Mr Colebrook.'

'That gives us an explanation without being a scrap of help,' Ian said gloomily. 'For the moment, then, we can only say that it seems highly probable that it's his corpse and wait for dental evidence.'

'I accept that,' she said thoughtfully. 'The dentist should be able to settle the question. But it leaves us with a problem. I, along with several other people, saw Mr Colebrook leave Tinnisbeck Castle, intending to head north towards his home near Edinburgh. There's no sign that he ever reached his home. His car turned up well on the way home. The car may have been wiped over, but I saw him myself putting on gloves before he drove off. If that was his habit, the few prints that were found in it are as likely to be those of a mechanic or his house-keeper's husband. His brace of pheasants was still on the floor behind the front seats. His gun and a cartridge bag were securely locked in the boot. The point I'm working round towards is that either he got into the water that evening and somebody else drove his car to the Bellbridge Hotel or he drove it to the hotel and somebody else brought him about halfway back towards where he started–' Ian began to speak but she held up her hand. 'Let me finish. He or the car may have done all sorts of journeyings in between, but the principle holds. What were you going to say?'

'You've just said it for me.'

'Don't thank me. How was the body found?'

A hospital porter on late duty. He usually gives his dog a walk before he goes to work. He phoned us and then went off to work like a good member of hospital staff but a thoroughly bad witness. I don't think he has much to tell us so I haven't had him fetched away from work. The finder is usually suspect, but in this instance he seems to have no connection whatever with the Colebrooks. We had a quick look around before the light went, but there are no obvious signs of violence. Probably Mr Colebrook was brought there to be disposed of. Unless, of course, he jumped in of his own accord or met with an accident, but the absence of his car makes either unlikely. I suggest that one of us might see him tomorrow while the other attends the post-mortem. And we'll have to have a better search of the banks of the loch. Not, I think, a full-scale fingertip search of the whole area unless something turns up to suggest that more than the simple dunking of an already dead body took place there.'

She nodded sadly. 'For all the good it'll do us after more than a fortnight of wintry weather. But I suppose somebody may have dropped a monogrammed handkerchief or a bloodstained dagger.' Privately, she wondered whether she would prefer to lead the search in the wind and rain or to attend the postmortem in a nice and dry but chilly mortuary.

The decision was made for her. 'I'd better attend the PM,' Ian said. 'You catch the porter before he leaves for work and then go round the perimeter with my two beauties.'

'How was the body dressed?' she asked.

'Tweed jacket and breeks, cotton and nylon shirt, Saltire Society tie, woollen sweater, braces, green kilt stockings and garters, brogues, cotton vest and pants. And a cartridge belt. We took that off rather than have live ammunition so easily available.'

'That sounds pretty much how I last saw him, except that I wouldn't know about his underwear. And it agrees with how his housekeeper says he left home. I'd like to see the clothes. Could I get a look at him before they undress him?'

Ian looked at her doubtfully. 'You won't like it,' he said, 'but I suppose that could be arranged.'

She was tired and the idea of facing the night again was unattractive, but she could imagine some eager beaver or an attendant arriving for work at some godless hour and making an immediate start. 'Could we go now?' she asked.

He looked at her in surprise. Then he nodded. 'I'll phone and make sure that there's somebody there to let us in.'

Ian's car was already locked away. They left Pippa in the house and took the Range Rover up to the hospital. A mortuary attendant produced the body, rather with the air of a conjurer showing that the lady was not in fact sawn in half. A body that has spent several weeks in water is not a pretty sight but Honey had become at least partly inured to unpleasant sights and was able to control her nausea. She studied it with care.

'It certainly looks very like him,' she said. 'The clothes look very similar, all but one thing. A pair of green Wellingtons was found in his car.'

'Is that the one thing?'

'No. The one thing is that he was wearing a cartridge belt. The loops were full? I thought so.' She probed cautiously at the corpse's waist. 'And his right-hand jacket pocket is full of cartridges too. You missed those.'

'He'd been shooting. You knew that. We'll empty his pockets in the morning.'

'He had shot quite a lot. So why was the belt full? And I'm sure that he never put cartridges in his pocket, he loaded from his cartridge belt. I'm positive that I remember seeing him take his cartridge belt off.'

'A belt of twelve-bore shotgun cartridges is heavy,' Ian said. 'So he was meant to sink?'

'Until natural processes brought him up again. He may have been meant to stay down.'

'Yes. Which confirms that he was put there as a method of disposal. I noticed one other thing. I can't believe that it's of any significance. His shirt was tucked into his underpants.'

She hid her amusement and then sobered as she saw the implications. 'That doesn't mean that somebody else dressed him. And it doesn't mean that they didn't, provided only that the somebody knew his personal habits. I don't think we need consider the possibility that he was killed at home and brought away again. Let's get back to the car.' When they were settled in the Range Rover again and rolling down the hill she said, 'I had to attend the autopsy when an MP committed suicide while I was in the Met. Between that and shopping for my father, I know a little about men's clothes as purchased and worn by old-fashioned gentlemen of English upbringing. The upper crust male, once he's past a certain age, dislikes anything that grips him around the waist. Belts, elasticised waistbands and self-supporting trousers become anathema. He likes everything to hang comfortably and, more important, reliably from the shoulders. So he wears braces, and his underpants have loops through which go the legs of his braces. I've even got Sandy sold on the style of dress for winter. Now think about it. With that arrangement, his shirt has to be tucked into his underpants.'

'Like they used to say laughingly about

John Major?'

'Yes. Thereby revealing themselves to have no aspirations above Marks and Spencer.'

Deborah met them at the door, along with an anxious Pippa. They each sniffed. 'You smell of the morgue, both of you,' Deborah said.

'You let your imagination run away with you,' Ian told her.

'Well, humour my imagination, both of you. Go and change. Get ready for bed and come down in dressing gowns for a nightcap.'

'If we're having a pyjama party,' Honey said, 'you must join in and not just serve the drinks, looking superior. Go and put on your frilliest nightie.'

Deborah laughed. 'No, thank you very much. The minister would certainly arrive at the door. And I'd hate to give him an excuse for his infuriating air of superiority. He puts it on so much more convincingly than I do.'

Chapter Twelve

Ian had to leave the house early. Business in a mortuary begins promptly, despite any lassitude on the part of the occupants in transit. Honey had a slightly more leisurely breakfast with Deborah and Ronnie, fetched Pippa from the back porch which she had shared with the Fellowes's Labrador, and set off to keep an arranged appointment with the finder of the body. The rain had gone and the wind had blown itself out, leaving a cool but pleasant day.

A B-road passed near the small loch where the unfortunate gentleman, whoever he might turn out to be, had been found. A rough track connected the two. Honey was first at the rendezvous but she had over-taken a motorcycle with a large dog seated, very upright and dignified, in a sidecar. This turned out, as she supposed, to be con-veying the hospital porter. The unmarked Ford bringing PCs Bright and McFadden followed on.

The dead man might have walked to the

waterside but more probably had been carried, alive or dead, by vehicle. Since then the porter, who introduced himself as Sam Wylie, had circled the loch a dozen times on his morning walks and, following his grim discovery, the scene would have been traversed by the ambulance, several cars and many more sets of feet. Nevertheless, she saw no need to risk disturbing any fragments of evidence that might conceivably have survived. They walked from the road. The track showed all the signs of traffic, vehicular, pedestrian or animal, but if any of it was of significance Honey could not perceive it.

Mr Wylie was insistent that she call him Sam although he was meticulous in addressing her as Inspector. A snap of his fingers brought his dog out of the sidecar. This was an absolute canine cocktail with no particular breed dominating. He was hairy, long-eared, short-nosed and bowlegged but nevertheless very appealing and biddable. Pippa, when brought out of the Range Rover, took one look, gave one sniff and accepted the other as harmless and well-intentioned. With a flicker of the telepathy that can develop between dog and owner, Honey thought that Pippa, as a pure-bred Labrador, was enjoying quiet amusement at the other's mixed parentage. The other dog, however, was quite unabashed and retained a manner both friendly and exuberant. Mr Wylie, though just as friendly, was round-faced and balding.

It was Honey's experience that quite different details may be noticed while travelling in one direction as against the other, so after a very short briefing she sent the two PCs to circumambulate the loch clockwise while she and Sam Wylie went round it widdershins. They were, she told them, to look for signs of activity and, though it was to be supposed that the dead man had arrived at the water by way of the track and entered the water thereabouts, they were to look particularly for any signs of traffic arriving at any other point.

The day had brightened and even the sun was making an occasional appearance. A mild breeze left over from the previous day's wind stirred the upper branches of the pines. The loch extended to no more than perhaps four or five hectares. It was a pretty spot. Trees had been kept back from the immediate waterside, presumably to aid the casting of an angler who cared to try for the one or two brown trout who snatched at the belated hatch of midges that still danced over the water.

From the appearance of the corpse, there could be little doubt that it had been in water for most of the interim since the day of the shoot. During that period there had been rain and a few hours of light frost, so she was not optimistic about finding a clear record. Sam Wylie pointed across the water to where gaudy tapes marked the spot where the body had drifted to the bank. Honey studied the tracks made by Mr Wylie's trainers, which he claimed to have worn every day for his walk so that he could change into clean shoes for work. The path around the loch was muddy in places. Mr Wylie's footprints were well represented, as were those of sheep, rabbits, dogs and, she was fairly sure, a fox but no tyre tracks or other human prints were discernible, so it seemed that any movements by officers or stretcher-bearers had been kept away from the path and on the short heather.

They moved slowly. Sam Wylie had made it clear that he had time to spare before his work. Honey was carrying her camera and was prepared to collect and record the location of every scrap of toffee paper or other rubbish but there was nothing to be seen. Even traces of animal origin were few and clearly nonhuman. There were even one or two hoof-prints of a horse, but the idea of Mr Colebrook being transported across a saddle, as if by some Valkyrie, was too much to swallow. The trampled area where the body had been lifted from the water was taped off, though she was at a loss to think what good that would do except to preserve a record of the churning of the mud by constabulary feet. The place, after all, had been randomly chosen at the whim of the wind and current and there was no reason to suppose that the dead man or any ill-wisher had ever set foot there. Sam Wylie was positive that he had never met another human on his daily walks there, except for one or two anglers in season. The season was now well past.

A few yards further on they met the two DCs. Bright and McFadden had nothing to show except for a carrier bag that they had retrieved from the water and which could have blown there from miles away.

They walked on.

'Anglers,' she said. 'Could you describe them?'

'Gosh, no. If a man's facing the water and I walk past behind him, I maybe say "Good morning" and he maybe answers but he doesn't usually look round – too busy watching his fly. And I maybe say "Any luck?" and all the reply I get is "Bugger all" if you'll pardon my French, Inspector. And it's a couple of months since the fishing stopped.'

'Have you ever seen two men at a time?'

'Once or twice.'

So the possibility of guests was there to confuse the issue. All the same, the point remained. 'Somebody had to know that this loch was here,' she said, 'but you can't see it from the road and it isn't marked on the ordinary scale road maps. If I send somebody with some photographs, could you pick out anybody that you've seen before?'

Mr Wylie scratched his bald spot. 'I could try. I'm not promising anything, mind.'

'If you promised anything, I'd know that I couldn't rely on you. Too many witnesses tell the police what they think we want to hear. What we do want is the truth.'

'There was one man who'd caught a whopper. Must've gone three and a half pounds easy. He showed it to me, more than once. I might remember him.'

'Was he red-haired and rather tall?'

'Short, fat and balder even than I am.'

They completed the circuit and met the

two detective constables again. An area of churned-up earth had been taped off near the mouth of the track but there was nothing to be learned from it. The forensic team had already been over it and, in making casts of whatever they hoped against hope might prove significant, had left nothing of interest behind. They began the walk back to the cars. Sam Wylie, who was becoming pressed for time, hurried ahead.

'Well,' DC Bright said, 'that was a perishing waste of time.'

'You think so?' Honey said.

Her tone warned him. 'All right, Inspector,' he said. 'So I'm an idiot. What did I miss?' They had worked together in the past and he knew just how far he could go.

'You saw the loch. Did you know that it was there?'

'Well, no.'

'You saw the fish?'

'A few brown trout. Nothing over about half a pound. Just tiddlers. What about them?'

'Big fish probably feed deep at this time of year. I have a little job for you,' she told him. 'Find out who owns the fishing here – if it's not free-for-all. I suspect that it's stocked. So is it a club? Or does somebody sell tickets? Is the local authority the landowner? Find out. I want a list of ticket-holders and I want photographs of them. And make it quick. Inspector Fellowes wants a briefing meeting at four, to follow the post-mortem as far as it's gone.'

'That's quick,' McFadden said.

'The local pathologist's abroad, skiing,' she explained. 'There's only a newly graduated assistant there, holding the fort. In view of the problems of working on a body that's been under water for several weeks, they've brought Professor Mannatoy through from Edinburgh. He can only spare the one day. What I want you to do is to gather up what photographs we have of everybody so far known to be connected with the case. If there's anybody we don't have photographs of, go and get sneak shots of them. Then show them to Sam Wylie. You won't be able to get through all that before this afternoon's meeting, but do the best you can. I want to know who knew that the loch is there. It may not lead anywhere, but we're very short of leads.'

'I don't fish,' McFadden said, 'but I knew there was a loch here.'

'Do it anyway,' Honey said through gritted teeth.

If there were to be a delay in solving the mystery of the body in the loch, the team would inevitably build up to the point of requiring a substantially larger incident room; but the recreation room in Newton Lauder nick that was usually taken over for the purpose was in use by a team from Edinburgh looking into a spate of indecent (though admittedly witty) emails deriving from somewhere in the area. The small team was therefore packed into Ian Fellowes's inadequate office. The last straw was the arrival, just as Honey's mobile phone warbled its tune, of DS Blackhouse. The superintendent, anticipating that the case was about to become one of murder, intended to take over but in attempting to enter he was frustrated for the moment by the fact that Honey was anxious to leave the room in order to take her call in peace and without disturbing the meeting. It would have been against his principles to retreat to allow passage to one of his subordinates, even a female and one as favoured as DI Laird. The team and the super were thus obliged to listen in frustration to one side of the call.

This was from Stella Weems, back at HQ and still following up, between other commitments, the responses to enquiries about the missing spaniels. What the listeners did not hear was Stella explaining that the two young spaniels had been identified, by their implanted microchips, at a boarding kennels in Fife. The proprietors had remained unaware of their identity until reminded by a client of the appeals for information. The listeners heard Honey say, on a rising scale of exultation, 'That's great... But who?... False name?... No description... Colour blind?... All right, leave it to me.' After a few more words, unintelligible to the listeners, she disconnected, smiling.

At this point she awoke suddenly to the fact that she was obstructing her superior's path and holding up the meeting. With a quick apology, she switched off her mobile, took a seat and gave the rest of the meeting only intermittent attention. Several vague ideas that had been tormenting her began to crystallise.

Mr Blackhouse usurped Ian's chair as of right.

Honey had encountered Professor Mannatoy in the past. The professor was a rotund, bustling little man, usually cheerful but given to bouts of irascibility. He was placed on the left of Mr Blackhouse with the assistant, a fresh-faced ex-student with the unlikely name of Blatt, beyond him. The other team members had fitted in as best they could.

DS Blackhouse introduced the professor, who had already consulted his watch more than once. The professor in turn introduced his assistant. It was immediately clear that no love was lost between the two.

'You'll want to know the result of the autopsy, as far as it's gone,' the professor said. 'I shall have to leave the remaining work to Mr Blatt, but it should consist of no more than routine and the writing of a formal report. The important facts are these. The deceased has been identified from dental evidence as Mr Henry Colebrook.' The assembled team acknowledged the confirmation of their beliefs in their own ways, by a nod or a grunt.

'The body was better preserved than is often the case, thanks to the rapid formation of adipocere due to the coldness of the water. He is said to be fifty-seven years of age and I saw nothing to contradict that. He was in good health except for the usual minor ailments to which we are all prone as we age. They will be listed in Mr Blatt's report – if you're lucky,' the professor added with a ferocious glance at the assistant, who flinched.

'The man had been dead and in the water for at least two weeks, perhaps longer, possibly much longer – I would hesitate to put an upper limit to it. He had not drowned – the amount of water in the lungs and air passages was negligible. From the petechiae discernible in the face and eyes – although Mr Blatt failed to remark them–'

'They're very faint,' the assistant protested just as faintly.

'Of course they're faint after this time in water,' the professor snapped. 'But they are nevertheless there. A pathologist has to make do with what is there, faint or not. Taken in conjunction with the presence of a scrap of feather in one of the air passages, they indicate that the deceased was smothered with a pillow. There were no other signs of violence and the hyoid bone was unbroken, so any possibility of strangulation can be discounted. And now,' he said, looking again at his watch, 'I am guest speaker at a dinner in Edinburgh this evening, so I must leave you. Mr Blatt can answer any questions. If his answers dissatisfy you, I shall be available by phone from tomorrow morning. I can come through again if problems arise. Thank you, gentlemen.'

Ignoring any attempts at questions, the professor squeezed between the chairs and made his escape. Mr Blatt could be seen to relax.

'This,' Ian said, 'is a whole new ballgame. There's no way, or none that I can think of, that he could be smothered with a pillow at the waterside. Either he made his way home after all or he entered another bed with somebody, presumably a sex partner, and was smothered there.'

Mr Blackhouse was not going to let a mere detective inspector steal whatever thunder might be going. 'Feather pillows aren't as common as they used to be. Forensics may be able to tell us more about it. Will you pass the feather to them?' he asked Blatt.

'Right away,' Blatt said. 'It isn't a whole feather, however. Just a tiny scrap.'

'Next,' the superintendent said, 'we need to know which houses use feather pillows. Fellowes, you can put that enquiry in hand. His own house and those of his sons, to start with. I suggest that we meet tomorrow morning to review the case.'

A moment,' Honey said. She paused for a second to pass the facts in review across her mind. 'Let's not go off half-cocked. If we start visiting houses to ask that sort of question, the guilty party will be warned. And I'm not saying that the premise is wrong, but do bear in mind that the family business is now concerned with meat products, pheasants in particular, so the presence of a scrap of feather in the airways could have another explanation. Mr Colebrook had just left the shoot. Also, though he very rarely went near the factory, one of his sons could easily have carried a pheasant feather into his father's car. Either way, Mr Colebrook could have breathed in the scrap of feather. I suggest that we wait for a report on the feather. Anyway, I have a lead but it's too tentative to discuss yet. Give me until morning to make some enquiries.'

If anyone else had dared to interrupt DS Blackhouse in that manner, the superintendent would undoubtedly have blown his top. Expressions chased each other over his face while the team waited, breathless, but his high opinion of her prevailed. 'Very well,' he said. He turned to the assistant pathologist. 'I suppose the symptoms of suffocation couldn't arise because he inhaled a piece of feather?'

'Not in my experience,' Blatt said.

'Right. Eight-thirty tomorrow morning here.'

Ian Fellowes felt a similar need to re-assert himself and he was still offended by Honey's reticence. 'One moment,' he said. 'Before deferring action, I want to know what this other lead may be.'

That was enough to stir DS Blackhouse's resentment on behalf of his protégée. 'Nonsense,' he snapped. 'The girl knows what she's doing. It can wait until morning.'

The team scattered, some to clear their paperwork, others no doubt to enjoy an early evening for a change. Honey, who had sat in on more autopsies than she cared to remember, intercepted Mr Blatt on his way to the car park. 'Are you going back to work?' she asked.

'The professor would expect it. So will your Mr Blackhouse.'

'So will I,' she said firmly. 'I suggest that you take some muscle tissue and put it under your microscope.'

'If you expect water to show up in the interstices–' he began.

'I don't. I'm thinking back to a case I was on in the Met as a junior detective constable.' She explained. His eyes widened.

On her way to Ian's house, she called in at the gun and fishing tackle emporium in the Square. Deborah's father, Keith Calder, was in sole charge. He knew Honey of old and gave her a nod before going back to talking technicalities with the owner of an expensive over-under twelve-bore. It gave her time to look at him. He was wearing better than most of his contemporaries. He had even kept most of his hair although it was definitely more grey than black.

'I'll add a little weight to the butt for you,' he said at last. 'After that, you won't feel the recoil and it'll balance better.'

The customer thanked him and made his departure. Keith bagged the gun and put it away carefully behind the counter. 'Now, Officer,' he said. 'What can I do for you?'

Honey begged him not to be an ass. They had known each other for years; indeed, at one time she had rented the flat over the shop. She asked after his wife before going on to ask the question that had brought her to the shop.

'That loch belongs to the Bracken Estate,' Keith said. 'It's let to an angling club. I'll give you the address of the secretary, if you like. I expect you've realised that any member could take a friend along as a guest, so you'll have a long row to hoe.'

That evening she was especially nice to Ian.

With Deborah's help she coaxed him back into a good mood without exposing her uncertain theories to the light of day. Over a light dinner she said, 'Mr Blackhouse has made up his mind that he's going to be a godfather to my baby. Who put that daft idea into his head?'

'If I find out I'll tell you.'

Honey smiled grimly. 'Don't even bother telling me. Just kill him for me. Or her.'

'Why don't you just tell him you don't require his service?'

'Why don't you tell him for me?'

'Good God no!' Ian said.

Before retiring, she sent an email to her friend Poppy.

I was delighted to hear from you that you thought that Jackie and Andrew were responding to your TLC. But now – whoopee! – I'm happy to tell you that Spot and Honey have been located in a boarding kennels. I am leaving them there for the moment rather than upset them by taking them into another interim home. Break the news gently in case Andrew goes off pop. Let me know when the couple can be expected home and I'll arrange to have the dogs collected.

She took both Labradors for a last walk under a clouded moon, cheerfully conscious that she had filled Andrew and Jackie with happiness and with a little luck she would have stuck a pin into Professor Mannatoy's self-satisfaction. She would have to drag all her theories out into the light of day shortly. Just what would be the repercussions if her theories were proved wrong she tried not to think, but she had kept her figure. She could probably go back to modelling.

Chapter Thirteen

By morning she had begun to doubt her own logic. In setting out for her early dog-walk she drove round by the mortuary. Two attendants were already at work but Mr Blatt was not present. He had worked late, she was told, and had then left to snatch a few hours of sleep. She would cheerfully have shaken him awake if she had known where he lived. She drove up to Moorfoot Loch but Pippa had to make do with a walk so rapid that she had barely time to empty herself. Returning, she failed to intercept Mr Blatt on her way to the meeting.

DS Blackhouse had stayed the night in the hotel and was taking up more than his fair share of Ian Fellowes's office as the team assembled. Blatt was the last arrival, squeezing in just as the meeting was about to begin. He apologised to the meeting and then, before his bottom had even settled into the chair, he asked Honey, 'How did you know?'

She breathed easily again. She opened her

mouth to reply but Mr Blackhouse got in first. 'Know what?'

'Inspector Laird suggested that I took a look at some muscle fibres under the microscope.'

'And you found?'

'Voids between the muscle blocks.'

The detective superintendent blinked at him. 'Meaning?'

'Meaning,' Blatt said, 'that he had been frozen.'

There was silence as those present tried to digest the news. Mr Blackhouse broke it. 'We've had some frosty weather...' he began.

'Nothing like deep enough and long enough to freeze a body,' Ian said. 'I think that Mr Blatt means that he had been preserved in a deep freeze.' He looked searchingly at Honey. 'That was a good question. How did you know?'

'If you mean how did I know about muscle fibres, the answer is that while I was with the Met I had to attend an autopsy on a woman. She had died of natural causes but her very wealthy father was also failing from the same degenerative disease. We discovered that it was well known in the family that he had willed his money to be divided between his surviving offspring. Her husband realised that if her apparent death was post-poned until after her father had popped his clogs, he would be very much better off. So he bought a chest freezer and postponed her apparent death until his father-in-law had fallen off the perch, by which time her share of her father's money had been gratefully received on her behalf by her husband. That's when I learned a little about the effects of freezing on the human body.

'On the other hand,' she said, 'if you mean how did I come to suspect that he might have been frozen, that's an even longer story.'

'That is what I meant,' Ian said. 'And you knew it. Tell us anyway, long or short.'

'It isn't a coherent story,' she said. 'More a succession of facts and hints that somehow added up to the outline of a story.' She paused. During her dog-walks she had gone over and over the facts and they seemed to have arranged themselves in sequence. 'As you know, I met, or thought I met, Mr Colebrook about three weeks ago. At the time, I thought that he carried his years quite well and somebody remarked later that he seemed to forget about the stiffness of age when something took his mind off it. Photographs of Mr Colebrook Senior taken at the time of his retirement show that his face had not changed its shape with age, not to the extent of a broken jaw-line, for instance. Instead of a few deep folds and wrinkles he had a network of small, shallow wrinkles. That would be very easy to fake, given a son who bore a strong family resemblance.

'My Mr Colebrook also made a special effort to be friendly to dogs. Mr Colebrook Senior was known to be a dog lover whereas each of his sons is nervous of them and avoids them if possible. I did some telephoning after the meeting yesterday. Until he retired, Mr Colebrook was often seen walking his two terriers but soon after that it seemed that his dogs were left to the care of his housekeeper.

'When I began to enquire into his disappearance I was told that Mr Colebrook had sold his own businesses about seven years ago and made large settlements on his sons who used them to establish their own business in partnership. That period of seven years struck me as being hugely significant. If he had lived until now, those gifts would have been tax free, but if he had died shortly after making the gifts they would have been subject to a heavy tax burden, probably more than the sons' newly established business could have stood at the time.

'I don't think that I ever met the real Henry Colebrook, but I'm told that of his three sons, Vernon, the eldest, in particular, bore the most striking resemblance to him. I was reminded by another case that it takes very little cleverly applied make-up to change the apparent shape of a face. The tiny wrinkles would have been fine lines drawn on the skin. In hindsight, I think that he had also added brown spots to the backs of his hands. He had added grey to his hair and changed the timbre of his voice. But, travelling in the Land Rover, I had found myself looking at the back of his neck, not concentrating but just seeing it because it was there. There was a pattern of three little red spots on the back of his neck, which I didn't see on the corpse but which I'd seen without quite recognising on Vernon Colebrook.

'I remembered another thing. The use Mr Colebrook Senior made of his cellphone ceased, according to his invoices, seven years ago. The only cellphone that we have been able to trace to him was not the pay-as-you-speak type. We assumed then that he had no need of a mobile phone after he retired, but there may be another reason why he stopped using it.

'Another coincidence. The two dogs that my Mr Colebrook seemed particularly taken with were the two young spaniels belonging to Andrew Gray and his partner Jackie Fulson. In retrospect, I think that he was not quite at ease with them and was forcing himself to befriend them, but that may be no more than hindsight. He was treating them to peppermints, to which both dogs are addicted. Just before he drove off from Tinnisbeck Castle, somebody mentioned that Andrew, Jackie and the spaniels lived just over the hill from his father's house. The house was bequeathed to Vernon Colebrook and he had let everybody know of his intention to occupy it when the time came. If he did so, he would be bound to encounter the two spaniels sooner or later. But he was well known to be nervous of dogs. Like the dogs, he is addicted to peppermints, in his case as an aid to not smoking. Dogs are not easily fooled by superficial disguises such as grey in the hair, make-up and an elderly posture. They depend more on sound and scent and the one thing they never forget is a source of edible treats. They would certainly recognise their friend with the peppermints.

If they made friendly overtures, as they undoubtedly would, it might set somebody thinking. The imposture was safe just as long as nobody began to question it.

'So the dogs were stolen that same night. To their credit, the brothers did not destroy the dogs. Perhaps they intended to arrange for their return once memory had faded. They have just been found, in a boarding kennels in the middle of Fife. Of the various kennels in the Yellow Pages for Edinburgh, it is the remotest one. Unfortunately the proprietor is colour-blind and couldn't say whether the man who left the spaniels for safekeeping was red-haired or not. Another of my phone-calls determined that Mr Leo Colebrook owns a diesel Land Rover which agrees with the noises that a neighbour heard that night.'

She fell silent and waited for derision to fall on her head.

It takes time to assimilate a new and radical concept. Ideas had to be turned inside-out. There was silence while minds turned over facts and theories. It was left to DS Bryant to break the silence by asking the awkward question. 'It's still not quite seven years since the gifts to the sons. Why would the sons kill their father before the period of seven years was up?' he asked, with an air of helpfulness that did not fool Honey for a minute.

It was a question that had been troubling her. 'Heavens,' she said lightly, 'you can't expect me to do all the hard work. You must do a share of the guessing.' Mr Blackhouse decided to laugh so everybody laughed. 'The seven years were almost up. The tax burden would be quite small and the business well enough established to bear the cost. But there's a lot we still don't know. If Professor Mannatoy's right about the petechiae, somebody smothered Henry Colebrook. Possibly one of the sons – there could have been a quarrel and a sudden loss of temper. Mr Blatt, would you really say that it's impossible for a man to turn over in bed, perhaps have a heart attack, breathe in a feather and choke?'

'Nothing is totally impossible,' Blatt said. 'I think that it's highly unlikely. I don't believe that it could possibly have happened in this case but I'll take advice.'

'I'm not convinced,' Honey said, 'that Mr Colebrook was murdered by one of his sons. I have no more to go on than a feeling that any son ruthless enough to kill his father and do the rest would certainly be quite ruthless enough to terminate a couple of spaniels. And in all the comments that witnesses have made about the family there has been no suggestion other than that they were all on excellent terms.' Honey paused and looked round the intent faces. They did not look disbelieving. She hurried on. 'Whatever had happened, whoever did the deed, they decided that their father must not die, officially, for another seven years, or however many were left out of the seven. So one of the sons was elected to take over and play both roles. That would be Vernon. Neither of the others is so perfect a match for his father.'

'The housekeeper would have to be in on the plot,' Ian said.

'That's for sure. This is all speculative – I'm mostly going by how I'd do it if I were in their shoes along with whatever supporting circumstances come to mind. Vernon, if he was the substitute, lived a withdrawn but quite credible life. It was simply given out that his father, now retired, was enjoying his very secluded existence and preferred to keep it that way. The father need only be seen, very occasionally, in the distance. His dogs accepted that going for walks with the housekeeper was now quite normal. As purchasing director, Vernon seldom if ever visited the factory – his function was to be out and about, striking deals with estates, shoots and game dealers. His dealing with the office staff and with the suppliers could mostly be by phone and email.

'When the seven years were almost up, they decided that their case might be helped and any later doubts assuaged if their father were to be seen around more often, but preferably not by anybody who had known him too well. So the impersonator went on a cruise and found himself placed at the same table as the Carpenters. He got on well with them. They invited him to their inaugural shoot. This was a safe distance away from Moonside House, yet they were a respectable group who could swear that Henry Colebrook was alive and well at that time.'

The room was flooded with silence as the men digested the story. There was some nodding. DS Blackhouse was on the point of speaking when the phone on Ian's desk rang peremptorily.

'Leave it,' the DS said, but Ian lifted the instrument and listened. 'Well done,' he said. He looked around the room. 'Forensics has moved swiftly. They put the feather under the microscope. It comes from a duck but not a duck ever seen in Britain outside a zoo or a special collection. It is oriental in origin, possibly mandarin or a close relative, strongly suggesting a pillow imported from Asia. It couldn't possibly have come off any bird being processed in the factory.'

'Or killed on the Tinnisbeck Castle shoot,' Honey said.

This time, Mr Blackhouse managed to pre-empt the discussion. 'We need all three sons in for questioning,' he said. 'And the housekeeper. Better get on with it straight away.'

'Before that,' said Ian, 'or simultaneously, I suggest that we need to search all four houses. An impersonation like that could never have been carried off without leaving traces. And we want fingerprints and DNA of the impersonator to compare with those of the real Henry Colebrook.'

'We also need to know what went wrong with the dental evidence,' Honey said. 'That is, if I'm not right up a gum-tree. That's one for you, Sergeant.'

DS Bryant sighed deeply.

'Simultaneously is the word,' Mr Black-house said. Honey recognised his change of attitude. His sole strength was as an organiser. 'Move against one of them and, if we've guessed wrongly, the guilty one could be far away or covering his tracks before we get round to him. This is going to take a lot of skilled searchers. Spend today thinking up the questions you want answers to. I'll drum up enough bodies to bring in four people to Edinburgh HQ and search four houses simultaneously.'

'I had assumed,' Ian said stiffly, 'that we would bring them here. This is the area in which the body was found.'

DS Blackhouse was not one to loosen his grasp on a case that seemed near to a solution. 'The probability is that any killing was carried out close to Edinburgh,' he said. 'All that happened in your territory was the dropping of the body into the water. Your team can go on looking for witnesses. But you, Inspector Fellowes, could come through and sit in on the interrogations if you insist.'

'Oh, I insist,' Ian said. 'I insist all right.'

Chapter Fourteen

Detective Superintendent Blackhouse, now that he had impressed his authority on the whole case, departed back towards Edinburgh in order, as he said, to drum up his teams for the morrow. There was a general air of relaxing, of sitting at ease or even undoing buttons.

Ian led them through other reports but without adding anything immediately identifiable as useful evidence. Casts and photographs had been taken of the area where the body had presumably entered the water, but only after the first officer to reach the scene after Sam Wylie's phone-call had backed his panda car to and fro over any previous tracks. Ian promised Honey the offending constable's head on a silver salver. No witnesses had so far turned up to provide any useful sightings at all. The secretary of the angling club had faxed in a long list of members entitled to fish the loch in season, but none of the names were so far known to have a connection with Henry Colebrook, his sons or any of their business interests. The nearest addresses were never less than ten miles from the loch, ten from Edinburgh and fifteen from Tynebrook village. If the immediate enquiries bore no fruit, a long road lay ahead – of visiting every member and asking who had been taken to the loch as a guest.

'Will the super be arranging any identity parades for tomorrow?' Honey asked. 'He was only talking about house searches.'

'Good point.' Ian's hands made a convulsive gesture as if to clutch his brow but he checked himself in time. A senior officer must never let his juniors see that he is fallible. 'I'd jog his memory, only I don't want my head bitten off if he's already put them in hand.'

'I could remind him for you,' she said. 'On the other hand, HQ is back on my territory. If I find that it's slipped his memory I'll arrange them myself. If it isn't practical to bring the kennel proprietor to Edinburgh, he'll have to pick out the man who left the spaniels from photographs.'

Ian looked happier. 'Right. Once we've hauled in the suspects, we'll have to move quickly or charge them. The disinterested and available witnesses who saw most of the spurious Mr Colebrook would be the Car-penters. We'll need formal statements from them anyway. You and the sergeant go through tomorrow morning, take their statements about meeting him aboard the ship and inviting him back to Tinnisbeck. Stay in touch by mobile, but unless we get a confession I'd expect to want them in Edin-burgh by mid-afternoon. Hannah Phillipson might also be able to pick out the false Henry Colebrook, so bring her along. Stay the night again tonight.'

'Thank you. I'll arrange to meet the wit-nesses tomorrow morning. Then I'll spend the rest of today tidying up the paperwork.'

'Fine.' He hid a smile from the subordin-ates present. 'You could include whatever it is you're not telling me about the Blakelove robbery.'

'I could,' Honey said. She never told him that she would.

'Fine,' Ian said again. He fanned himself with a blank report form. 'There's a hell of a fug in here. Somebody open a window.'

Bright threw open one of the centre-pivot windows just as McFadden opened the door. The ensuing hurricane blew papers all over the floor. Some of them even made it along the corridor.

The next day was Friday and Honey had every intention of spending the weekend with her husband, who was due home on the late train. She packed up her chattels with care, thanked Deborah for the hospitality, discussed a few minor points with Ian over breakfast and got on the road in good time with Pippa in the back and DS Bryant sitting at her side, nursing a small holdall and a grudge. It was another bright, crisp morning.

Bryant was emitting waves of disapproval. 'I thought you wanted me to check out the dentist's evidence,' he said.

'I wanted you to do that yesterday,' Honey retorted grimly. She postponed asking him what he had been doing instead, preferring to keep that up her sleeve. 'Do it as soon as we've finished here.'

On their previous journeying she had shown the sergeant that she could drive at speed. This time, she decided to let him see that she could drive more slowly without letting her attention wander. She stayed well within the speed limits, signalled meticulously, cornered with care and gave other drivers more than their due share of courtesy and consideration. The sergeant showed no sign of relenting in his fervid disapproval of women drivers and could be seen to tense every time another vehicle appeared around a distant corner.

As a result of this caution, they were slightly behind their intended time when they reached Tinnisbeck Castle. She decided on a short cut. 'They're expecting us,' she said. 'You go in and take a formal statement. You know exactly what we want. I'll go and collect Hannah Phillipson.'

He looked less sure of himself. 'You're the one who knows the ins and outs of it,' he said. 'I could go to fetch Miss Phillipson.'

She had no intention of letting him drive her treasured Range Rover again. 'They'll tell you the ins and outs,' she said. 'You'd never find the place.'

'You could give me directions.'

'I could not. I'm none too sure of finding it first time myself. You're supposed to keep abreast of the ins and outs. This will give you a chance to catch up.'

She turned the Range Rover and drove off before her temper could get the better of her. Pippa made small sounds of displeasure at being carried away from one of her favourite places. Honey, still seething, stopped at the gates and let Pippa out to stretch her legs and have a pee.

The smallholding seemed to be dozing in the sunshine. It looked deserted until Gemma Kendal appeared suddenly around the end of the building. She was dressed workaday, in jeans and a baggy sweater, and she seemed nervous. 'Come to the sewing room,' she said. 'Hannah's expecting you.'

Honey shouldered her bag and followed. The garden, she noticed, was becoming depleted as the vegetables were consumed or preserved. The big workroom was comfortably warmed by bottled gas heaters. At the far end, Hannah Phillipson was seated at the sewing machine. Despite the unhandy nature of the treadle machine she was running seams with confidence and mastery. 'One minute,' she said. 'Then I'm with you. I don't know that I can help you much. I hardly spoke to the man. Thank you, Gemma.' She finished her seam and cut the thread with a small pair of scissors.

'She does lovely work, doesn't she?' Gemma said grudgingly. She had ignored the implied dismissal in Hannah's words and retired only as far as the doorway.

'She certainly does.' But Honey spoke absently. She was taking in what she was seeing and not quite believing it. The material was a superfine cream silk with an unusual pattern woven into it but barely visible. The exquisite French panties in the machine were undoubtedly to the design that Julian Blakelove had picked out of the encyclopaedia. Another part of her mind was recalling that Pippa had recognised a friendly scent at Hollington House. She felt the prickling up her spine that came whenever she sensed the arrival of a breakthrough. 'How many of these sets have you made?' she asked.

'This is only the third,' Hannah said. She covered the sewing machine. 'A lady I know – who shall be nameless – brought back a length of the material from Thailand, folded in the bottom of her suitcase. She was given it as a special favour by one of the local nobility but–' Hannah winked '–she wouldn't tell me what she did to earn the favour. She also provided the paper patterns. I made it up for her in return for the rest of the length and the patterns. This is almost the last of it – it's for a lady in Hawick. The length ran to three sets and there's enough left for one more. Gemma got the second set. I owed her for nursing me through a really bad bout of flu last winter.'

'So there won't be any other sets to match, anywhere?'

'Only the ones I've just mentioned. It would have to be a hell of a coincidence, this silk and this design. I repeated the designs for a lady in Newton Lauder, but that was in pale green nylon. And I can't think where you might get some more of this silk, except back in Thailand.'

Honey turned towards Gemma, but she had vanished. Honey cursed herself. Unlikely though it might seem for exotic lingerie to be recognised, and from a description by a man, there would be no other obvious explanation for her own sudden interest and Gemma might have taken fright. Honey darted out of the building. The back door of the house was bolted. She blessed herself for having locked the Range Rover. She had not seen any other car around. Presumably Cruikshank was away with the Land Rover. As she came near the house she could hear Gemma's voice somewhere, but too muffled for her to make out the words. The front door was unlocked.

The sitting room was very dark after the brightness outside. As her eyes adjusted, she saw that Gemma was just putting down the phone. Gemma turned defiantly.

'Who were you calling?'

Gemma shook her head.

Honey fished a pair of handcuffs out of

her bag. They were not very ladylike hand-cuffs but they would do. Honey had no intention of putting her baby at risk by allowing the other space to fight. Gemma struggled but she was no match for muscle and long practise. She was soon firmly attached to the arm of a heavy chair.

Hannah arrived, panting. 'What on earth's going on?'

'Listen and you may find out,' and to Gemma, 'I'm arresting you on a charge of being concerned in a robbery.' She added the statutory warning. As she spoke, she was keying Last Number Redial. A voice came on the line, saying something about not being available. She pushed the phone at Hannah as the voice continued, inviting the caller to leave a message after the tone. 'Whose voice is that?'

Gemma was trying to signal warning messages but the bemused Hannah failed, or perhaps refused, to register them. 'That sounds like Pat Kerr,' she said.

'I thought so.' The voice had definitely not been that of Johnny Cruikshank. 'Now stand back and don't interfere. That isn't my only pair of handcuffs. Your friends seem to have been indulging in a little robbery. In fact, this charmer seems to have used the pretty things you made for her to seduce a wealthy householder while her lover entered his house.'

Hannah collapsed into another chair. 'Never!' she said.

Honey did not bother to reply. She keyed her mobile phone but without result.

'You won't get a signal here,' Hannah said. 'Too many hills round about. You'll have to use the landline phone.'

'I thought you were my friend,' Gemma said bitterly. 'Whose side are you on?'

Hannah looked at the other without affection. It seemed that an early friendship had not survived the stresses of sexual rivalry. 'It isn't a matter of sides,' she said sadly. 'I hope I never have to choose between friendship and law and order. At the moment I'm only being helpful to the police. If being helpful to the police means that I'm being unhelpful to you, that's too bad. I've no sympathy for anyone who can't abide by the law. If you don't like the rules, don't play. I'm sure the inspector will pay for the call.'

Honey was already on the phone and speaking to Newton Lauder. She gestured to Hannah to sit down and stay there. With the whole strength of Newton Lauder CID scattered, it seemed quickest to speak to the uniformed Superintendent. 'I need some backup,' she said. 'I have one of the couple who robbed Julian Blakelove QC here. The other is a Pat Kerr of Tynebrook village. He'll be out driving the baker's van at the moment and I want him pulled in before he gets home and listens to his answering machine in case the haul disappears again, if it hasn't already been fenced. And somebody should listen to the messages on the machine. I want one or more woman officers to take this prisoner off my hands. And I want two houses searched. We don't have time for warrants; this is urgent if we want to recover some very valuable jewellery and paintings.'

There was a moment of stunned silence on the line, but Superintendent Dedridge had seen her at work before. 'I'll have to ask Edinburgh for help.'

'I doubt if you'll get much in a hurry. They have four houses to search there and I think they've drawn off what there is of your local CID to participate. Please, Superintendent, see if you can find me several intelligent officers from the uniformed branch.'

She heard him sigh. 'Honey, I hope you know what you're doing. How sure are you?'

When she came to think of it, she was stirring up the whole ants' nest on the basis of some high quality but definitely erotic underwear. She said that she was sure, while praying that he was not going to ask the crucial question. But she had got on very well with Superintendent Dedridge during her first stint in Newton Lauder and again when cases had brought her back to the small town. She thought that he rather fancied her and probably fantasised about her when he was alone, which was quite acceptable as long as he did nothing to pursue his fantasy. A little erotic imagining in somebody else's mind did her no harm.

'I know you wouldn't go off half-cocked,' he said at last.

'Certainly not, sir,' she said, infusing her voice with sincerity. 'One other thing. I'm supposed to be taking two witnesses to Edinburgh about a different case. Would you let Superintendent Blackhouse know that I'm held up here. I'll send the witnesses in with DS Bryant and for the moment I can be reached only on this number. As soon as I can move, I'll be available on my mobile.'

She disconnected and found that her hand was shaking. She was quite used to thinking of more than one thing at a time, but this was definitely Over The Top. Her mobile might not be working but at least it could be used to remind her of the phone numbers she wanted. At Tinnisbeck Castle, Hazel Carpenter answered the phone.

'I'm held up on another case. Would you mind conveying Detective Sergeant Bryant to Edinburgh? He can direct you. How many would your Porsche carry?'

'We do have another car,' Hazel said.

'In that case, perhaps you'd also carry another witness with you. Hannah Phillipson. Put the sergeant on, please. Hullo?'

DS Bryant's voice came on the line. 'Hullo. What can I do for you?'

'You go into Edinburgh with the Carpenters.'

'In your car?'

'No, not in my car. In their car. But come here first and collect Miss Phillipson. Perhaps I'm wronging her, but Miss Phillipson might be tempted to make life difficult by warning somebody, so keep her away from a phone until you hear from me.'

'I can do that.'

The self-satisfaction in his voice made her want to say that he'd bloody well better, but she restrained herself. 'Get going as soon as the Carpenters are ready,' she said. She disconnected. Her mouth had gone dry at the thought of being wrong and having to explain how she had come to leap to the wrong conclusion. She turned to Hannah, who was looking mildly amused. 'You can move around now,' she said. 'And I think we could all do with a cup of tea.'

Hannah got up. 'You could have trusted me,' she said.

'I expect so,' Honey said. 'But I had to be sure.'

Chapter Fifteen

Within fifteen minutes, the Carpenters' dark green Volvo arrived at the door. Warning Gemma Kendal to make no attempt to escape on pain of unspecified sanctions, Honey unplugged the phone and took it with her as she accompanied Hannah outside. Hannah's smiling but unhelpful parting words to her erstwhile friend were, 'I told you it was Friday the thirteenth,' to which Gemma replied by calling the other a fat-arsed bitch. It seemed that relations that had already been cold between the two had now become arctic, which in turn suggested that Hannah's testimony might be freely given but perhaps not without bias.

There are no rules against a simple business transaction with a witness, so she drew Hannah aside for a few moments to enquire the price if the remaining piece of silk were to be made up from the patterns but to her measurements when unpregnant. A deal was struck. The price seemed to Honey to be quite favourable. Hannah must have been in a good mood at the prospect of being rid of her inconvenient companion and having the undivided attention of Johnny Cruikshank.

Returning to the house secretly smiling at having a delightful extravagance in prospect, and one whose cost Sandy could not possibly guess, she invited Gemma to make a clean breast of it. The invitation was rejected in two short words, only one of which would have been suitable for use in polite company.

Superintendent Dedridge must have been pulling out all the stops. The Volvo was hardly out of sight before a Vauxhall from Traffic arrived bringing two other officers, one of them a tough-looking female sergeant. Honey was happy to deliver the sulky Miss Kendal to them along with a warning that no phone-calls were to be permitted until further notice.

Almost a further hour passed before the arrival of a large Ford laden with constables under the charge of another sergeant, this time a man with a moustache. It also brought Constable Picton, with Dancer. The delay allowed her time, while treating Pippa to a quick but overdue walk, to plunge again into uncertainty. Identical silk could easily have been brought back in the suitcase of some other tourist who would then have been mad not to choose top-of-the-range patterns. Only the recollection of Gemma's attitude reassured her. Surely only the guilty would behave that way. But guilty of what?

She began the search of the house and found and admired Gemma's copies of the silken underwear, carefully laundered and folded in tissue paper, but a spare part of her mind was busily fretting over innocent reasons why Gemma Kendal might have bolted to the phone. The new arrivals took her mind off it by demanding orders as to what they were to look for and where. They also passed a message that she was to get down to the village as soon as possible to instruct another group which would arrive there within the next half hour, or an hour at the most. At least her memory was working satisfactorily. She was able to reproduce the list of goodies stolen from Hollington House almost word for word. She told them to look absolutely everywhere. And if either John Cruikshank or Pat Kerr, or any other male unable to account for himself, should turn up, he and his vehicle were to be searched while he was to be held incommunicado. She also stressed that the house was the home of a presumably innocent witness whose evidence would be valuable in two separate cases. The house should not be thoughtlessly damaged or unnecessarily disturbed but should be left as tidy as when they entered it, or preferably tidier.

The sergeant seemed to know what he was doing. She warned him that he was in a dead area for radio and that if they needed her they could use the landline phone to reach Control, who could then pass a message via her mobile, or phone her mobile direct.

Once she could be sure that no hole or corner of the house or outbuildings would be missed, she drove the few miles to the village. She could see little for a trained dog to do at the smallholding whereas there might well be a man to arrest in the village; and if Superintendent Dedridge was getting desperate, her next reinforcements might have been culled from the typing pool. In the village, there was no sign yet of the promised officers, of Pat Kerr or of the baker's van. She parked outside the pub. She found Ian Argyll behind the bar but, on hearing what she wanted, Ian handed over the duty to a woman in a floral pinny and came outside with her. It took him only a few seconds to release the catch on one of the sash-and-case windows and climb inside. Another half minute saw him relock the window and emerge through the front door. She slipped inside.

The message on the answerphone was short and to the point. *That policewoman's here again*, said Gemma's voice. *She suspects something, maybe everything. Pick me up at the corner of GledWood and don't forget to bring the goodies.*

Little though she liked being referred to as 'that policewoman', she felt a huge glow of relief. Those few words confirmed that she was on the right track. Examination of the machine showed it to be the type with a small cassette of tape, which she impounded.

Leaving the door on the latch, she returned to the pub. Suddenly she was hungry. Her car outside the door should be a sufficient indication to her colleagues of where to find her. Lunchtime was almost over and the bar emptying of its few customers but she persuaded the woman in the floral pinny to provide her with a large portion of lasagne, which she started with relish while watching from a front window. She had made little impression on her lasagne before a people-carrier pulled up at the door.

Hurrying out, she found an elderly inspector from Traffic, two female constables and a civilian employee. Superintendent Dedridge was indeed scraping the bottom of a very limited barrel, but the inspector was rather looking forward to a change of responsibilities. The good worker makes use of the tools to hand and at least they had been provided with overalls. She led them to Pat Kerr's house and set them to searching. Regardless of creases to her own tailormade wool suit, she borrowed a set of overalls from Ian Argyll and joined in.

In one sense the work went well; in the other, it was a disaster. Every corner of every cupboard was examined. Each possible container was opened. Surfaces were studied in the hope of seeing signs of secret hidey-holes. The garden was examined carefully, but if the goods had been buried the weeds had been carefully replanted on top. Her spirits fell. Either the haul had already been fenced or it was hidden somewhere else. There were miles of winter-vacant fields around where a short-term interment would be safe. Or, of course, the pair was innocent. Perhaps that phone message referred to something completely different, something of which Honey as yet knew nothing, and the wicked were fleeing when Honey was not in fact pursuing.

The only possibly compromising item found was locked in a cupboard, the lock of which yielded to amateurish picking. It was a double-barrelled shotgun of Spanish make, almost exactly as described by Julian Blakelove. Word from the smallholding, relayed from Newton Lauder, reported that nothing whatever had been found. When another call advised her that Pat Kerr had been intercepted by a traffic car when he had already finished his round and was now on the way home, her feelings of anxiety only increased. She might even be right in all her assumptions but her head would be just as surely on the block if she could not come up with some supporting evidence.

Another message came through Newton Lauder and her spirits recovered a little. The premier fence in Glasgow, who was being interrogated about some stolen Japanese pornography, had attempted to curry favour by revealing that he had been approached, only the day before, with an anonymous enquiry as to whether he would be interested in Mrs Blakelove's jewellery. He claimed to have indignantly denied any interest but his story was backed up by enough circumstantial detail to compel belief.

The baker's van, preceded by a traffic car, drew up at the door. Pat Kerr was escorted into the house. The traffic car was driven hastily away to resume its patrols – which was understandable, she thought. With so many of the traffic and other uniformed personnel being tied up helping her, Superintendent Dedridge must be hard put to it to cover all of his considerable area of responsibility.

Pat Kerr was predictably angry, though Honey could see definite signs that he was playing it up. She interviewed him in the kitchen with the traffic inspector present. Kerr wanted his solicitor summoned. Very well, Honey said bravely, call him. He was totally innocent, he insisted, and knew nothing about any robbery and was barely acquainted with Gemma Kendal. The shotgun was properly recorded on his certificate.

As his protestations continued, she became ever more certain that he was lying. He had begun to sweat. His eyes met hers at the wrong moments and the small movements of his hand ceased just when she was sure that he had departed from the truth. It was only when he thumped the table and kept reiterating that she had found nothing, nothing, that her mind slipped into overdrive again. There was one place yet to be searched.

'I am going to take you into custody,' she said. 'I'll see that the van gets returned to your employer.' He prepared to speak but then clamped his jaw shut. 'Shall I give the leftover loaves to your pig?' she asked.

His face changed, switching suddenly from macho to pathetic. 'I'll do a deal,' he said.

'No deals. You have nothing left to deal with. Come outside.' Her only set of handcuffs had gone in to Newton Lauder gracing Gemma Kendal's wrists. She led the way out, keeping a close eye on her suspect. Kerr's dog was beside the driver's seat of the van, in defiance of the rules of hygiene but presumably to protect the day's takings. The dog had met Honey before and perhaps recognised her as an authority figure. It came out peacefully enough and was put on a spare lead. Holding the dog, Honey sent in the visiting traffic inspector and the civilian employee. Pat Kerr was now sweating heavily and showing signs of panic. There was no secure vehicle handy for confining him so she kept hold of him. The van, they reported, had been swept clean but at the back on a low shelf were several loaves. They brought one out to her and she rapped it with her knuckles. It was as hard as concrete.

The traffic inspector, who was getting into the spirit of the hunt, suggested opening one of the loaves which showed signs of tampering.

'All right,' she said. 'But not a large white – there are two paintings that could be rolled up inside but they couldn't put it back in the oven without risking the paintings. Try the small wholegrain.' She handed over the prisoner to the traffic inspector and broke open the small loaf on the tailboard of the van. It was found to contain two necklaces, two bracelets and a selection of rings.

In the moment of triumph the little group focused on the gems. It was Pat Kerr's chance. He jerked his sleeve out of the traffic inspector's hand and bolted. Honey grabbed for his arm, and missed. He hurdled the nearest fence and set off across the grassy field towards a thick wood. Most of the party dashed after him but it was immediately clear that Kerr had a fine turn of speed that the representatives of law and order, being sedentary or older, were quite unable to match.

Honey and Constable Picton were accustomed to having their pursuits done for them by those bred and trained for it. The two dogs were in the back of the Range Rover, only a few yards away. Honey lost her grip on the lead holding Kerr's dog but it took only a second or two for Pippa and Dancer to join the party. They saw the receding figures. They received the word of command. And they were off. It was neck and neck.

'A fiver on it?' Picton said.

Honey felt that she had to back her own runner although a Labrador bitch was ill matched against a male German shepherd. 'You're on.'

The chase was on in earnest. Kerr's dog tried to jump the fence but the lead was caught up and it was held there, yelping and barking in turns. Figures were spread over the field. Pippa and Dancer recognised the furthest figure as the fugitive and tore between the stragglers. Honey recognised for the first time what the poet had meant by *the rapture of pursuing*.

At first the German shepherd took the lead and Honey resigned herself to the loss of her fiver. A hare rose up from under Kerr's feet and Pippa, who had very definite ideas about hares, looked set to tear after it, but she decided that the man was a more attainable or a more worthy subject of the chase and returned her attention to the original quarry. Dancer was well ahead but at the last moment he trod on a sharp stone and limped almost to a halt. Pippa dashed ahead. Kerr looked over his shoulder, saw a large, black dog bearing down on him and tried to put on a spurt, but he trod on a loose clod, his ankle turned and he fell headlong.

Honey was handicapped by wearing the wrong shoes. When she came up, breathing heavily, Pippa was sprawled across Kerr's chest and licking his face with a huge, wet Labrador tongue.

Chapter Sixteen

Though she was elated by a successful day, as her exhilaration wore off Honey had to admit to herself that she was tired out. A day spent doing everybody's thinking for them, while at the same time expecting disaster and humiliation, followed by the letdown from the adrenaline rush had exhausted her. She could have borrowed the same bed again from Deborah and Ian Fellowes, but she had already said her farewells and duty still called. Moreover, she was longing for a return to her own home and her own bed with her own husband.

It was some little time before she could turn the Range Rover in the direction of Edinburgh. First, she had to reverse her activities of the day. The two houses had to be left lockfast, the officers returned whence they came, Pat Kerr formally charged and delivered to the custody officer for onward transmission to HQ in Fettes Avenue and she had to thank Superintendent Dedridge for his unprecedented degree of cooperation. She also had to prepare a brief report on the day's occurrences, skipping lightly over the skimpy evidence on which she had made her moves but leaning heavily on the evidence now available.

Luckily the Range Rover was equipped with a hands-free telephone kit. As she drove, she tried to reach Ian Fellowes, but he was still busy with the witnesses and suspects in the case of Henry Colebrook's strange death. She left a message asking him to call her back. Then she phoned home. Sandy had not yet arrived but his plane had landed. He had phoned June to say that he was ravenous and would very soon be home and in need of a meal. She gave June a message for him. She would be late and she might be busy on the next day, so he could fix himself up with a day's golf if he wished. On Sunday she would be his and would expect him to be unequivocally hers. She disconnected. The light rain had resumed, making driving into the dark against the lights of commuter traffic a penance. She would not have fancied golf on the morrow, but the weather might change and anyway men were different. They enjoyed getting cold and wet and muddy, she told herself. It was what they were *for*.

Five hellish miles later, when sleet had increased the difficulty of driving, the phone sounded. She expected the call to be from Ian but Superintendent Blackhouse was on the line. He had received his copy of her report by email and was loud in congratulations. The baker's van had reached Edinburgh and the proceeds of the robbery seemed to be complete and intact. She had better come in to HQ and attend while the QC identified both the lady and the loot. She could then complete the formal charges.

She was entering Edinburgh by way of Gilmerton when Ian called back. He sounded as tired and fed up as she felt. Although any crime could be presumed to have taken place outside his territory, the body had been found well within it. Any questions of territorial boundaries were resolved, because Detective Superintendent Blackhouse, who knew no boundaries, had nominal charge of the case; but it was the super's habit to delegate any tasks requiring hard work or deep thought to selected underlings. His own participation tended to consist of administration, at which he was good; interference, for which he had a special talent; and usurping any credit at the end of the day. At that last, he was a genius.

The bulk of the interviews had been left to Ian, who had divided most of the day between the three brothers and their house-keeper, without obtaining any significant admissions from any of them. Whether any of the house searches had proved worth-while would not be known until the results of forensic reports and DNA tests were delivered.

'I'm on the way in,' she said. 'I'll see you in about fifteen minutes.'

First she called at home, to deliver Pippa to June with instructions to feed her. At the thought of food, even dogfood, she was over-come by the hunger that was to be expected after a long day of hard work with only a partial lunch. Her favourite carryout was almost on the route. She decided on one of her occasional lapses from the dietary regi-men that, along with her perfect metabolism, accounted for her continued slenderness. She phoned ahead and a polystyrene box of scampi and chips awaited her at the shop. She ate while she drove, her eyes watering with pleasure, and cleaned her fingers on a paper towel from the glove compartment.

When she arrived in the small office that had been put temporarily at Ian's disposal she was neat and presentable and bearing some papers and two cups of coffee. DS Wylie, dapper as ever, was closeted with Ian but she let him fetch his own coffee.

While the sergeant was out of the room she asked Ian, 'How do you get on with him?'

Ian sat up and stretched. He was comfortably dressed in slacks, an open shirt and a loose sweater and his hair was tousled. Honey usually preferred tidy men but she was tired of the sergeant; Ian's informal appearance topped by his square-jawed face and fair but unruly hair was more to her taste. 'He's good,' Ian said, 'but not as good as he thinks he is. All in all, he's a pain in the bum. He thinks he should be the inspector, not me.'

'And you have the advantage of being a man. He thinks a woman's place is in the home. Try to keep him out of my hair. How's the interrogation going?'

'We've seen the housekeeper twice and each of the brothers once without extracting any admissions. Just a lot of *no comments* alternating with flat denials. I'll let you read the transcripts when they're produced but you won't be much the wiser.'

Sergeant Wylie returned and seated

himself. He had moved his chair a little closer to Ian's as if to align himself with a fellow male against the intrusive woman.

The papers in her hands she had collected from her own desk on the way by. She scanned them quickly while she spoke. 'One thing puzzles me,' she said. 'How did his dentist come to identify the body? How long had the imposter been going to that dentist?'

Ian sifted through his own papers. 'If it gives a date here, I can't find it.'

'I thought the sergeant was going to find out,' Honey said.

DS Wylie nodded. 'I'll enquire in the morning.'

She narrowed her eyes. 'You'll do it now.'

He looked at his watch. 'But–'

'Do it,' Ian said. His voice, usually calm and measured, had suddenly developed barbs. 'And get on with it. If he changed his dentist within the last seven years we want to know who his previous dentist was and we want his dental charts from that time. We want to know who is his more recent dentist and we want those charts. We also want to know who gave us the outdated name of his dentist. Was it an innocent mistake or deliberate deception?' The DS looked at his watch again. 'Do it now,' Ian snapped. 'Dentists will be heading home soon and we need that information first thing.'

The DS got to his feet and left the room, every inch of his back registering wounded dignity.

'I could have dealt with him,' Honey said.

Ian smiled and nodded. 'I know you could. I saved you the bother. We have the brothers and their housekeeper in the cells and we can hold them until tomorrow without any difficulty. Where do we go from here?'

Honey yawned and gave half a shrug. 'I haven't got my thoughts sorted out yet. All I have is a host of discombobulated hunches. I keep thinking that timing is at the root of the whole thing. Why did the body make its appearance just when it did? Why did my least favourite QC get robbed at about the same time? Are the two things associated or is it a coincidence? The robbery must have been in planning for weeks or months, so what triggered it? When is he coming in, by the way?'

'He's here now,' Ian said. 'He came straight from court. I'd arranged for somebody to show him the recovered items for identification. Mr Blackhouse was collecting suitable females for an identity parade.

If he picks her out–'

'He will,' Honey said. 'No question about it. At least, I'm assuming that he looked at her face. And then we'd better question her while she's off balance.'

'We'll have to get a formal statement from Mr Blakelove.'

'You can do that,' Honey said. 'It will be your chance to ask him how we got onto her in the first place.'

Ian brightened. 'I could certainly do that. And the kennels owner is on the way, bringing the two spaniels with him.'

'While we're waiting,' Honey said, 'you could ring Deborah. I see that the sleet's turned to serious snow and it'll be worse over the Lammermuirs. By the time we're through here it will be late and we'll need an early start in the morning. Tell Deborah that we'll give you a bed for the night, as a repayment of your hospitality to me. While you're doing that, I'll send another email to my friend Poppy. I want to know when she's putting Andrew and Jackie on a plane home.'

Honey returned to her own desk while Ian saw the QC; and there the two spaniels duly arrived, climbing all over her as an old friend. The man from the kennels was elderly and stooped. He wore thick-lensed glasses, but nevertheless Honey was soon delighted to hear that he had picked out Leo from a line-up of red-headed men as the client who had deposited the spaniels with him. She made a fuss of them before depositing them in the care of the dog unit.

She found a note on her desk when she returned, to say that Ian and Mr Blakelove were waiting for her in Ian's temporary office. There had been another successful identity parade and Gemma Kendal had been recognised.

The QC still wore the black jacket and formal attire of his profession and his jowls bulged over the starched collar. Now that he was well slept and had recovered the missing goodies without his delicate secret being flaunted to the world, he was loud in his praises. He insisted on shaking her hand although without troubling himself to stand up. 'Such a clever young lady,' he said. 'I knew that she'd be the one to pull it off if anybody could.' He seemed to be congratulating himself on his reading of people and prediction of the future. And,' he added, 'I like to think that my own powers of observation made a contribution.'

Honey had no intention of being patronised by the elderly and fat. 'And did you tell Inspector Fellowes just what you observed in such meticulous detail?' she enquired.

The QC turned red and made a strangled sound for which his stiff collar may have been partly to blame. Before he could find his voice Ian chipped in. 'No, he said nothing about it. Perhaps now would be a good time to let me know just what was the subject of your feat of memory and description.'

Mr Blakelove coloured more dramatically. 'I have your promise,' he said.

'You have,' Honey confirmed. 'But you must see that, unless we get a confession, it may be necessary to transfer the young lady from the dock to the witness box and let the jury see her just as you saw her. If you were defending her, you would certainly want to enquire into the validity of your identification of her in the recent identity parade. Such matters as how her hair was dressed, how she herself was dressed and what makeup she was wearing would all be highly relevant.'

Honey's tongue was firmly in her cheek but Mr Blakelove, being overly sensitive on the subject, missed it. There could be no doubt that he took her point, nor that the picture of Miss Kendal parading in court just as he had seen her, and of himself being invited by hostile counsel to explain exactly which features of her attire had enabled him to set the police on her track, held no appeal. He heaved himself to his feet. 'I look to you,' he said, 'to avert any such event by obtaining a confession. Don't bother to see me out. I know my way around this building, have done for years.'

Ian had also risen. 'But rules are rules,' he said. He led the QC out but returned in a few minutes. 'The old fool wouldn't say a word. I'll get it out of you, one of these days. Come along. Miss Kendal's on her way to an interview room. It was your collar so you take the lead.'

Gemma Kendal was waiting in an impersonal interview room under the cold eye of a woman sergeant. The fluffy sex-kitten was looking older and considerably subdued. Any sexual allure that she possessed was not noticeable. Honey and Ian took seats across the table from her. Gemma wanted to speak but Honey waved her to silence. 'Your turn comes in a minute,' she said. She started the video and two audio recorders and recited the date and time and the names and ranks of those present. Then she said, 'You have already received the statutory warning. Would you like to hear it again?' Gemma shook her head. 'Very well, then. I am about to charge you with complicity in the robbery of Julian Blakelove QC on the 23rd of October last. Have you anything to say?'

As realisation of her predicament sank in, Gemma's manner had become less vitriolic and more wooden. 'I don't even know what you're talking about,' she said coldly.

Honey was beginning to enjoy herself. She was waking up. Now that she was on firm ground she could relish aping the manner of an advocate in court. She adopted her pompous voice. 'Then I shall enlighten you. Mr Blakelove has just identified you as the lady who begged a lift from him on the pretext that her car had broken down and was then in the process of seducing him when a man entered on your heels. Was the seduction completed, by the way, or was it frustrated by the intervention of your accomplice?'

'None of your damn business.'

Honey looked at her but decided that the words did not quite constitute an admission. 'Mr Blakelove was threatened with a shotgun. He was tied to a chair while you two opened his safe with his own keys and made off with the contents of the safe and two valuable paintings from his walls. That haul has now been recovered and identified. It was hidden in the van driven by your partner, Patrick Kerr, who is also now in custody. Does that refresh your memory?'

'It doesn't ring any bells.'

'Then let's see if we can't start any bells chiming. You were given a meal on arrival here and the mug and utensils that you used have been sent to the laboratory. We expect to recover samples of your DNA. We have the car that was stolen and which you were using when you entrapped Mr Blakelove and we have also recovered the very fancy underwear that you wore on that occasion. Your DNA will probably be detectable on the car seats. It and that of Mr Blakelove will certainly be detectable on the under-wear.'

Gemma Kendal produced a creditable sneer. 'Don't hold your breath,' she said. 'The stuff's been through the washing machine since then.'

Honey matched the sneer with a smile. 'Since when?'

Gemma could be seen to be thinking hard.

She must have realised that her words had turned a difficult position into a hopeless one. 'I'll tell you this much,' she said. 'I was driving the car. A friend had lent it to me. I'm not going to tell you his name and I didn't know that it had been stolen. It broke down in the rain and Mr Blakelove was kind enough to give me a lift to his house while I waited for the garage to send help. He rather fancied me and I was grateful to him. We were just beginning to have sex when a man followed us in with a gun and anything I did after that was under duress. If Mr Blakelove tells it differently it must be because he was under stress and getting muddled. I was scared that I'd be implicated so that's why I didn't go to the police. I'm not saying another word until I have a solicitor present, except,' she added spitefully, 'that sex with him turned out to be like being raped by an overweight and sweaty warthog and you can quote me on that.'

'Oh I will,' Honey said. 'Don't for a moment think that I won't. Now tell me the name of the garage that was supposed to be sending you help.'

'After I've seen my solicitor.'

'It would carry more weight if you told me now.' Miss Kendal shook her head in silence. 'Very well,' Honey said. 'And would you care to explain the message that you left on Patrick Kerr's answering machine? It is recognisably in your voice and I expect a voice print to give confirmation sufficient for a court of law.'

When they had left the prisoner to the care of the custody officer, Ian said, 'So that's what the fuss was about.'

Honey pretended to peep coyly from behind the papers in her hand. 'He's a bit sensitive about the fact that he could describe so precisely what she was wearing underneath. He only agreed to cooperate after I promised to be as discreet as circumstances allowed. It was the accuracy of his description that gave her away. There's one thing I don't understand. Once he was sure of having his property returned, why didn't he just say that Gemma Kendal wasn't the woman at all? She'd have got off and he'd have lost nothing except revenge.'

'I think he was going to,' Ian said. 'He hesitated and then spoke up almost defiantly. Spitefully too. Once he was tied to that chair, I think she may have said or done something to him that was so totally beyond the pale that he was ready to risk humiliation rather than let her get off.'

'You're probably right.' They covered the length of the severe corridor while Honey thought it over. 'We'll see if her story can stand up when we've interviewed Pat Kerr,' she said at last. 'My bet is that it doesn't have a snowball's chance in hell, but we'll see how Kerr shapes up. I can't see them having had the forethought to rehearse a story in which she's acting under duress. I just can't imagine Kerr going out of his way to prepare an escape for her that would only be needed if he got trapped. He doesn't have that much altruism.' She yawned. Tiredness was returning, coming over her in waves. 'Is Hannah Phillipson still here?'

'I think so. She made and signed her statement. Now she's waiting for a lift home.'

'From you?'

Ian had been infected by Honey's yawn. 'She'll be out of luck if she is,' he said when his own yawn had relented. 'No, I think there's a traffic car going south shortly, if it can make it. Otherwise we'll have to arrange accommodation for her.'

'Was she asked specifically about Gemma Kendal's evening absences during the period before the robbery, the times she got dotted up? And did they only happen on rainy evenings?'

Ian frowned. 'I think that that question was only raised implicitly.'

'I think it's an important point. Let's find her and quiz her about it. Then I suggest that we leave the whole boiling lot to stew in custody until morning.'

'I can't quarrel with that.'

Chapter Seventeen

Following her scampi and chips supper, Honey was not in the mood for another meal at home. She pleaded exhaustion and took to her bed, leaving Ian and Sandy to shoptalk downstairs. She slept like the dead, totally unaware of anything at a conscious level; but her subconscious must have remained hard at work because she awoke before dawn to find that, among all the facts and suppositions of her current cases, a dozen or so seemed illuminated like pin-pricks of light in a black night. In her dozing state they seemed to arrange themselves, clustering together as if revealing small streets and hamlets. Small, half-seen patterns merged at the edges...

Suddenly she was wide-awake and the activity in her mind made further sleep unthinkable. She slipped out of bed and began to dress. The intuitive reaction that grows between perfect partners told her that she was being observed. She looked round. Sandy was watching her with one eye; the other still buried in the duvet. He made a small sound expressing both admiration and lust. She smoothed down her dress, stooped and kissed him on the ear. 'Tonight,' she said. 'I promise.'

'I shall enjoy–' Sandy began. He was asleep again before he could finish the sentence.

She was scribbling a note for June while bolting her cornflakes when Ian slipped into the room. 'I heard you start moving around,' he said softly. 'If you're going back to HQ, I'm coming along.'

She nodded and smiled. The right words were refusing to come. 'Help yourself,' she said. 'There's tea in the pot. Just don't talk about the case yet until my hunches have sorted themselves out.'

Half an hour later, they were parking in adjacent slots. There had been a light snowfall and the snowploughs and gritters had left most of their route crisply white. All too soon the street verges would be stained by soot and grit but for the moment it was pristine. Before dawn on a Saturday there was very little other traffic. The Range Rover took the slippery streets without difficulty but in her mirror she could see Ian's hatchback wagging its tail. She slowed until he caught up. They walked up to Ian's temporary office together. It was cramped but at least they had more privacy than would have been the case in Honey's shared space.

Some members of the team had worked late or through the night and there were fresh reports on the desk. Dawn was coming up outside the window before Honey put down the telephone, straightened her back and said, 'Yes. I think I see my way. I told you once that I thought timing was the crux of this case and now I'm sure of it. There has to be a reason why things happened in the sequence and at the times that they did.'

Ian looked up from a file. 'Which case?'

'There's only one. Well, one and a half.'

'Now you're being deliberately abstruse.'

'I may be mystifying myself as well. Has anybody told the Colebrook brothers about the pathologist's report?'

'I gave explicit orders that it was not to be mentioned yet. As soon as they know that it's a case of murder, they'll clam up.'

'You're not as daft as Deborah makes out. So we have a fifty-fifty chance of their still being in ignorance. They're not exactly unclammed now,' Honey pointed out. 'In fact, I think the reverse may be true. Mention of murder at the right moment may open them up, but the moment will have to be right. Follow my lead and if I start to be hard on a witness you can jump in and play the good cop. Right?'

'Right. We start with the most vulnerable?'

'No. I think we let the housekeeper stew for the moment. If Vernon Colebrook has had his breakfast, let's see him now. There must be an interview room free at this time of a weekend morning.' She picked up the phone again. It was still warm from her previous calls.

Vernon Colebrook was waiting sullenly in the interview room, in the care of a uniformed sergeant, when they entered. Ian went through the preliminaries. Vernon listened patiently to a reiteration of the statutory warning. 'That's all right,' he said. 'Because I am not saying a word until my solicitor is present.'

'No lawyer takes calls at this time of a Saturday morning,' Honey said.

'I made my phone-call last night. He promised to be here early.'

'That's perfectly all right,' Honey said cheerfully. 'I'll do the talking and you can listen. Then you'll be able to tell your solicitor exactly what you're up against. The body that was recovered four days ago has been identified as that of your father. But it is not the body of the man who has been impersonating him for the past nearly seven years. That, Mr Colebrook, was you.'

Vernon roused suddenly and then subsided. His face had begun to collapse and his eyes had clouded as if in death. He cleared his throat but remained silent.

'You were about to remind me of the dentist's identification,' Honey said. 'But in our innocence we had referred to Mrs Mc-Laghan, your father's housekeeper, for the name of his dentist. Further enquiries reveal that the dentist who produced X-rays matching the teeth of the corpse had not attended that patient for more than seven years. Before that time your father had attended faithfully every six months. We have been unable to find any record of any dentist treating your father since then, yet the corpse's teeth were his own and corresponded exactly with X-rays taken seven years ago. We should all be so lucky as to need no fillings over such a period. You may care to save us some time and trouble by telling us the name and address of your dentist.'

There was no answer. Vernon Colebrook was looking blankly over her shoulder.

'We have just been on the phone to the factory. Even in the absence of yourself and

273

your brothers, your staff is arriving at work. It appears that there was a clearout of secretarial staff around seven years ago. Your father's secretary was given early retirement. Her replacement is being invited to come and attend another identity parade. I think that she may well recognise you as the recent occupant of Mr Colebrook's shoes. I myself sat behind the putative Mr Henry Colebrook in the Land Rover on the Tinnisbeck Castle shoot and I noticed that he had three small spots or freckles on his neck, in a roughly triangular pattern, just to the left of his spine and above his collar. Those spots were not present on the corpse but I recognise them on you. There is no doubt in our minds that your father died shortly after making the gifts to you and your brothers with which you started your business. The tax burden would have crippled you. You therefore froze his body and this is confirmed by the pathologist's report.

'One of his sons took his place. You are the son most strongly resembling your late father in face and voice. Your father's face had changed shape very little as he aged. The network of fine lines would easily be simulated in watered ink; and greying of the hair would be no problem at all. Moreover, as the buyer of the firm your place was out among the shoots and the big estates. I would not expect any current member of staff to be quite sure of distinguishing you from your late father. But there was little risk, because it was given out that your father was leading a very reclusive life in retirement. It is also noted that your father suddenly stopped using cheques and operated almost entirely by cash and credit card, thus averting the need to sign cheques. We have obtained some recent credit card slips of yours and several purporting to have been signed by your father and the signatures are remarkably similar.

'You live alone and your small house is in a rather isolated situation. Your father's house is similarly rural but is overlooked from the farm and from the factory. It would therefore be necessary for you to spend much time and most nights there, to be seen coming and going. Your absence from your own house would be largely unobserved but we are checking on your milk deliveries. The bedlinen and your father's clothes are being sampled for DNA and we shall see whose DNA makes a perfect match. Mrs Mc-Laghan is also in custody. The impersonation could not have happened without her full knowledge and participation. How long do you think she will hold out under questioning?'

Vernon was sweating and his face was drawn but he was pulling himself together. 'I have no comment to make until my solicitor is present,' he said shakily. 'Except to say that I would like a cup of tea.'

'Your mouth going dry?' Honey said. 'As well it may. Yes, I think we're all due a little refreshment.'

'I'll go,' Ian said. 'Tea all round is it?'

As the door closed behind him Honey said, 'I shall continue. When the seven years was almost up, it was nearly time for your father's death to take place. Another few weeks and the inheritance tax burden would have been lifted altogether. As it is, it will be very much reduced.

'You were preparing the ground for his official death. The discovery of his body might carry more conviction if he were known to have been walking around and meeting people shortly beforehand. You were still wary of anyone who might have known him well enough to detect small differences in appearance or gaps of memory, so you went on a cruise, mingling with many people who had not known your father. You became friendly with the Carpenters. Discovering that you also lived in southern Scotland and to the south of Edinburgh, they invited you to their shoot. It seemed to be far enough from your home to be safe so you accepted. It was pure bad luck that a young couple who lived near to Moonside House also attended and even worse luck that, to bolster the indications that your father rather than yourself was present, you made a great fuss of the two spaniels. As the party was breaking up, you discovered that they lived just over the hill from your father's house, which had been left to you and where it had long been understood that you would ultimately take up residence.

'The dogs would betray you. You are known to be nervous of dogs but you had been forcing yourself to feed the spaniels snacks and especially the peppermints to which they are addicted. Your mind may have been exaggerating the danger, but it seemed to you that a pair of strange dogs fawning over a man who was known to dislike the whole canine species might initiate an undesirable train of thought. So the dogs were stolen and lodged with the remotest kennels to be found in the Edinburgh Yellow Pages. Your youngest brother, Leo, has been identified as the man who brought the dogs to the kennels.'

'Leo knew nothing,' Vernon said huskily. 'He was only doing me a favour.'

'I see,' Honey said. Inwardly, she was smiling. Once a silent suspect opens his mouth, she thought, the thin end of the wedge is already inserted and only needs to be wiggled about a bit.

Ian returned, followed by a civilian employee with a tray bearing four cups of tea. He settled down to listen.

Honey resumed. 'Perhaps you could help me with something else, unconnected with this case and reflecting no discredit on any of you as far as I can see. In going through your father's older papers we came across a cheque, dated before the imposture began and made out to Cash. No other cheques from that period were preserved – indeed, I think it dates from after banks stopped returning cancelled cheques unless by special request – but this one had been put into a plastic envelope and placed in his filing cabinet in a folder of its own. There is no such person as Cash and so the banks don't usually require a countersignature on such a cheque. In this instance they may have been suspicious, because the cheque is signed on the back. The signature is a scrawl and appears to be Patrick Hale.' She paused for a moment. Another faint bell was ringing somewhere on the border between her conscious and subconscious thinking processes. For the moment she couldn't pin it down. 'An expert gives an opinion that the cheque has been altered. Can you tell me anything about it?'

For a moment it seemed that Vernon was going to abide by his policy of unhelpfulness. Then he shrugged. 'Not a lot,' he said. 'I remember him being angry because he'd given a building tradesman a cheque for some work done and the cheque had been altered and cashed. His anger was mostly against himself, for leaving spaces that a forger could slip extra words into, but he had written it out of doors, in a hurry and on a cold and windy day, so I suppose his carelessness was understandable. He was going to go to the police about it, but the man had vanished and Dad wrote it off to experience and thanked his stars that the amount hadn't been larger.'

'Do you remember the man?'

'I don't think I ever set eyes on him.'

Honey was interrupted by the arrival of Vernon's solicitor, a portly man that she had never previously encountered. Several more questions remained to be asked but she had got most of what she wanted and could infer the rest. 'We'll leave you two together for a client conference,' she said. 'I'll rewind the tape and start it playing and you'll get a copy later. The sergeant will be outside the door and when you've heard it through you can tell him and he'll stop it. There are no other listening devices.' She pressed the STOP and then the REWIND keys on one recorder and the STOP key on the other.

Outside the door, they looked at each other. 'Pat Kerr next, I think,' Honey said. She put her cup down on a windowsill; a habit that she knew would annoy the staff. 'I've just remembered something.'

'Remembered what?'

'Mrs McLaghan's maiden name. Let's have a word with Mr Kerr.'

Ian seemed about to protest. Then he shrugged. 'Whatever you think. You've had the lead in these cases. I'm just along for the ride.'

'Bless you for the generous soul that you are. Tell me when you feel ready to do some of the hard work.'

Ian looked at her hard. 'I've known you for a while, Honeypot. I've seen the penny drop before. You've just seen something. Did Vernon tell you something I missed?'

'Pay attention,' she said, 'and all will be revealed. Most probably the fact that my guesses have missed the mark and I'm making a bloody fool of myself.'

Pat Kerr, dark and macho as ever, was soon brought to another interview room. He refused the services of a solicitor on the grounds that that profession was usually on the side of the law and therefore no friend of his. He was ready, at first, to explode but it seemed that his anger stemmed from anxiety. He calmed when Honey explained that his dog was being cared for by George Brightside.

'The court may insist on appointing a solicitor to represent you,' Honey said. 'In any case you ought to have somebody to ... to paint you in your best colours. In the meantime, I suggest that you listen and when I've finished I'll ask you one or two questions which, as you know, you don't have to answer.

'It's my opinion that you don't have a hope of beating the charge of robbing Julian Blakelove. That, however, is only my personal opinion and you can draw your own conclusions after you've heard what I have to say. As you know, we found the proceeds of the robbery hidden inside stale loaves in the van that you've been driving for the baker. I suppose that you could argue that somebody hid it there without your knowledge, but you can see for yourself the difficulty of making that stick. In addition, you fit the general description of the male robber given by Mr Blakelove and in your house we found a shotgun answering his description of the one used in the robbery. Over the coming period we will be searching for your DNA in the stolen car and studying your movements in the time leading up to the robbery when Mr Blakelove's habits and movements must have been studied very closely. Your accomplice, Gemma Kendal, is also in custody and charged.

'You probably also know that courts tend to go easier when the accused has pleaded guilty and saved the considerable cost of a trial. Have you any comment to make so far?'

Pat Kerr shook his head.

'I'll take that as a no. Since you made the change from being a witness to being a suspect, we have been trying to complete your record on file. We know a little about your past few years. What you told me in a previous interview appears to be generally true. But so far – and I admit that this is an unpropitious time – we have been unable to find any record of your birth. In fact, you do not seem to have existed until your return to your present home. You must have changed your name. Tell me, what is your real name?'

Pat Kerr shook his head again.

'Was it Patrick Hale?'

Kerr twitched. There was another, more violent headshake.

'We'll take that as another no. I think that's what it was. Tell me, what relation are you to the late Mr Colebrook's housekeeper – whose maiden name was Hale? Remember, we already have samples of DNA from each of you and it will not take long for the laboratory to establish the relationship.'

All right,' Kerr said hoarsely. 'So she's my sister. So what? There's no law against having a sister.'

'No indeed. So your name was originally Hale. I suspect that under that name you committed a fraud by altering a cheque given you by Mr Colebrook Senior in payment for some small building work. Mr Colebrook had preserved that cheque. Do you wish to make any comment at this time?'

'No, nothing. Nothing at all. I'm fucked

283

if I do.'

'You could be right, Mr Hale. But you could find yourself in even more trouble if you don't. You met a man who you took to be Mr Colebrook Senior at the Tinnisbeck Castle shoot and you thought that he recognised you. That night the man disappeared and four days ago his body was found floating in a loch not far from his route homeward. Now do you have any comment to make?'

The prisoner's eyes were bulging and he had turned very white. 'You don't think I killed him?'

'No, I don't,' Honey said. 'But that's just a personal opinion. You can see how it might look in a courtroom. I'll leave you to think it over. You may decide that it's in your best interests to help us to pin the crime on the guilty party.'

Outside the room, as they headed for the lifts, she said, 'I feel just as guilty as anybody else around here. He doesn't have much to contribute, but in common justice I should have told him who's guilty. I'm assuming that he doesn't know. But the law didn't require me to tell him.'

Ian had stopped listening. 'When did Deborah say that I was daft?' he asked her.

Chapter Eighteen

Honey paused at a window to look out. The sun was breaking through, turning the snow into a blaze and reflecting enough light to throw their confused shadows onto the ceiling. All along,' Honey said, 'I had a feeling that timing was crucial to these cases and that they were linked. Didn't I tell you that I was sure there was a reason why things happened at those times and in that sequence?'

'You did. Several times. I see part of it,' Ian said, frowning. 'But you'll have to explain.'

'I will. But not yet. I'm not quite sure enough. I want to confirm something.' The sergeant was still waiting patiently outside the other interview room. 'The solicitor's still in with Mr Colebrook?'

'Yes Ma'am. They called me in to stop the tape, that's all.'

'Thank you, Sergeant.' She opened the door. Ian followed her into the room. 'It's Mr Walters, isn't it? I'm glad I've caught you. I have some more questions for your client and I think it may be in his interest that they're asked now and in your presence.'

The solicitor's eyebrows went up but he said, 'Very well.' He sounded almost relieved. Honey guessed that he had not been enjoying his client conference.

She started both tapes again and recorded the resumption of the interview and the presence of the solicitor. 'First,' she said, 'now that you've had a chance to confer, does Mr Colebrook wish to add anything?'

Mr Walters was looking worried. 'Not at this time,' he said.

'All right. That's his privilege.' She paused to add emphasis. 'The case has a more serious aspect even than fraud and concealing a death. Now is the time to tell you that the pathologist's report, in addition to revealing that the body had been frozen, reported on the cause of death. You will be given a copy of the PM report later, but it seems clear that Mr Colebrook Senior died from asphyxiation. The presence of a scrap of feather in the airways suggests strongly that he was smothered with a pillow.'

There was a total silence in the room. Sounds began to filter in from outside – voices in the building and traffic outside, but distant and muffled. Honey could hear her own heartbeat.

'The feather could have come from the factory,' the solicitor said, as if hoping against hope.

'I'm afraid not. The feather had originated on a bird of oriental origin. It could never have been processed in the factory.'

Vernon Colebrook leaned forward suddenly. The solicitor made a gesture as if to restrain him. 'No. I must just say this,' Vernon burst out. 'If this is true, it is inconceivable that I or either of my brothers would do such a thing. We were devoted sons.' He paused and rubbed his face. Honey could guess that he had not slept well. 'We didn't fawn. We didn't live in his pocket or spend hours on the phone to him, but we were genuinely fond of him and grateful, and I think he knew it. He had been father and mother to us since our mother died, twenty years ago. What's more,' he added suddenly, 'it would have been against our own interests. We were all right as we were. We would have had little to gain under his will.'

'And a tax liability if he failed to live just a little longer,' Honey said. 'As far as we have been able to discover, none of you has any financial difficulty.'

Vernon paused. He tried to control his expression but there was on his face, Honey thought, an expression that might well have been seen on the face of a man trying to pass a lump of coke. 'Yes,' he said at last. 'We manage very well. We don't gamble or whore around. We're not addicted to fast cars. The business is thriving. It pays each of us an income more than adequate for our personal needs. And that's all that I wanted to say.'

Honey was nodding. 'That's understood. My present inclination is to believe you. But you must see that in the state of present knowledge you and your brothers must be suspect. It seems highly probable – virtually inevitable – that you will be convicted of concealing your father's death. By the time that we have in all the forensic evidence and all the witness statements, I think that it will be inevitable. That, of course, amounts to an act of fraud against the Inland Revenue as well as being a crime in its own right. You must know better than I do whether you can now manage to pay the due tax plus interest and any fine that may be imposed. Nor could I guess what penalty the law may impose for concealing your father's death.

There is a more serious case to consider.

'Whether on present evidence and evidence still to come one or more of you would be convicted of his murder would be mere speculation.' Honey paused and then spoke with heavy emphasis. 'What I want you to consider is this. If nobody else is ever convicted of killing your father, the taint of patricide will linger around you and your brothers forever.'

Vernon seemed about to speak, then turned to the solicitor. Mr Walters blew out his cheeks and then said, 'I shall have to consult my client. Clients, I should say. I am also representing Daniel and Leo Colebrook. I ... I did warn them that conflicts of interest might arise and that in that event I would have to suggest the names of other solicitors for two of the three brothers.'

'Take your time,' Honey said. 'All the parties concerned are in custody at the moment and charged in connection with concealing the death of Mr Colebrook Senior. I need hardly point out that the police would vigorously oppose bail while the possibility exists of a more serious charge following. However, there is one matter, which I do not believe to be hostile to your clients, and which I believe would help them in the matter of that charge. I want fuller details of the fraud committed against Mr Colebrook just before his real death took place. I refer to the altering of a cheque. You have already given us a brief account.'

'This isn't a trick?' the solicitor asked.

'Of course not. This discussion is being recorded. No court would accept evidence obtained by any such deception.'

'Oh, for God's sake,' Vernon said. 'Anything, if it will only get at least one of us out of here. Our business still has to be run.'

Mr Walters considered. 'Very well,' he said at last. 'Go ahead. I'll stop you if we seem to be straying onto dangerous ground.'

Vernon took a little time to arrange his thoughts but it was clear that he was prepared to be open. 'About seven years ago,' he said, '–and as to the date I'll go along with whatever it says on the cheque – my father paid a mason a matter of about seventy pounds by cheque. The man had carried out some repairs to paved paths at Moonside House. The cheque was duly presented. At the request of the builder it was made out to Cash and it was taken in cash. At that time, the bank was in the habit of returning all cancelled cheques to the issuer. My father noticed that the cheque had been altered to increase its value by eight hundred pounds.'

When Honey said nothing, Ian cleared his throat. 'If your father complained to the police I'm surprised that we didn't uncover the complaint during our enquiries.'

Vernon managed a faint smile. 'My father consulted his solicitor, a Mr Hunterton of Edinburgh. He's dead now. Mr Hunterton's advice was to try first to recover the money. The man had moved away but his previous landlady had a forwarding address. The sum was substantial but not enormous and the threat of legal action might have persuaded him to make at least partial restitution. My father's death followed closely after that and, with his testimony not available, the family preferred to forget about the matter.'

'And all this was within the knowledge of your father's housekeeper?' Honey asked.

The atmosphere in the interview room changed. There was surprise. There was hope mixed with relief. Questions hung in the air. But Vernon stuck to the facts. 'Yes, definitely,' he said. 'I remember my father complaining bitterly in her hearing about the breach of trust.'

Honey paused. 'And neither you nor your father knew that the man concerned was her brother?'

Vernon's eyes opened wide. His expression of surprise was convincing. 'Was he? We never knew that. She certainly never let on.'

Honey was satisfied that if Vernon had already known of the relationship he would have mentioned it sooner. 'Years later,' she said, 'he returned to the place of his birth. Did you ever see him again?'

'Not to my knowledge.'

'He turned up as a beater on the Tinnisbeck Castle shoot. At that time, he was going under the name of Pat Kerr. A dark-haired man, badly shaved, with a spaniel-collie cross dog.'

Vernon shrugged. In his relief he was almost smiling. The solicitor spoke quickly. 'My client does not admit that he was present at that shoot.'

'You may come to see that it would be to his advantage to make that admission, once you accept the strength of the other case.' She turned back to Vernon. 'You exchanged a look with him. Yours may have been a casual glance. You may only have been returning look for look. But Mr Kerr thought that he was being recognised by the man he had defrauded. He decided to disappear again. But first he gambled on the time it would take for your father to decide to act, to consult the police and for the police to gather the facts and move in. He may have been ready to fly at short notice or to bluff it out if the police moved more swiftly. He had to wait a week for the weather that he needed to coincide with the necessary behaviour on the part of his victim. Then he carried out the robbery that he had been planning for some time. That could have financed quite a lengthy disappearance. But he did not repeat his vanishing act – probably because he then learned that Mr Colebrook Senior had disappeared.'

The solicitor was nodding slowly. 'I take your points,' he said. 'Allow us a little time for consultations. As you pointed out, there is little urgency – except with regard to the management of the business interests of my clients.'

As soon as Honey had stopped the recordings, Vernon Colebrook said, 'I want to assure you that none of us treated our father or his body without respect.'

Ian Fellowes was hot to interview Mrs McLaghan (née Hale) but Honey pointed out that the housekeeper was not going anywhere, whereas lunchtime had arrived and was about to depart. They headed for the canteen and settled in a quiet corner.

As they ate, Ian said, 'What did you make of his last statement?'

'Make of it? I think he wanted to say that whatever they had done with his father's body it had not been done lightly or casually but with as much reverence as could be managed in the circumstances. And I think he was trying to say that what they did was only out of dire necessity and that it haunted them and will haunt them for evermore. But perhaps I'm reading too much into a few halting words.'

'No, I don't think you are.' Ian ate reflectively. When he had cleared his plate he said, 'I get the picture now and I see what you meant about the sequence. Let's see if I've got this right. Your prisoner Hale, alias Kerr, was a bad hat. He worked as a mason but he wasn't above pulling a fast one on the side. He did a job for Henry Colebrook and altered the cheque. His sister, Mrs McLaghan, knew that Mr Colebrook was about to have Hale arrested. She also knew that she was mentioned in Mr Colebrook's will, so she smothered him, starting while he slept, but she's a strong woman with some weight to her. She told the brothers that their father had died in his sleep.

'The brothers were horrified. They had just spent their father's gifts on establishing a very promising business and to be called upon suddenly for the full amount of estate duty would have crippled them. So they decided to keep the old man alive. The members of staff who would have had immediate contact with the boss were changed and Vernon was elected to double up as Mr Colebrook Senior. No doubt the forensic team will find traces in a domestic freezer at one of the four houses.

'Vernon Colebrook took over his father's life, keeping out of the public eye but also being seen around as himself. He must have been a busy lad – no wonder he looks tired.

After nearly seven years, by which time the business was on firm ground and the tax burden greatly reduced, they were not so vulnerable. They were preparing the ground for producing the body, possibly in a fire, and passing it off as freshly deceased, when they were overtaken by coincidence. They could see great danger in the continued impersonation of Henry Colebrook so close to young neighbours and more particularly to their dogs who might well recognise in Vernon the man who they had met as Henry Colebrook. They decided that Henry would be seen no more and the two dogs were stolen and kennelled far away – instead of being destroyed, which suggests that the brothers were not without compassion.'

'That's about it,' Honey said. 'I must go and ask whether the spaniels have been collected yet.'

'You could go and do that,' Ian said. 'Have what remains of your Saturday off. You've done all the work so far, and very subtly too. Let me pretend to deserve a little of the credit. It's high time that you were taking it easy, in view of your delicate condition–' he grinned suddenly '–not that you show any signs of delicacy. You can leave me to finish off the interviews and get formal statements. I think the Colebrook brothers will see the advantage of admitting the lesser offence in order to have their father's murder placed squarely where it belongs. You'd think they'd have wondered why she was so willing to go along with the impersonation.'

'I expect they did. But it's amazing how blind people can be when their own ends are being served.'

That evening she wrote to her friend Poppy:-

I phoned home but the weather had cleared and

Sandy had gone off to his golf. He couldn't possibly be playing golf in the snow, could he? I dare say that the nineteenth hole is seeing a little action. The dog unit confirmed that the two spaniels, Honey and Spot, had been taken away, along with a bottle of Champagne that I brought from home and left for collection. The sergeant said, 'They were both in tears,' so I couldn't resist saying, 'The dogs?' I was in rather high spirits, you understand. He looked at me as though I was mad, which probably I was.

I decided to pay a visit to Thack an Raip *and see how they were settling in, hoping that a little happiness would rub off on me. The country roads were very bad but the Range Rover coped.*

The first thing to catch my eye was the figure of the unpleasant Mr Gloag, almost hidden in the snow-covered escallonia bush beside their window. I was going to give him a shock that would make him jump out of his horrible and insanitary skin, but the snow was crunchy underfoot. He heard me coming and hurried off round the house in the opposite direction. Before chasing after him, I wondered what he had found so interesting.

Honestly Poppy, I don't think that you need worry about your ex any longer.

On the hearthrug before a recently lit log fire, the two spaniels were curled up together. The two humans were fondly contemplating the snoring bundle of dogs while entwined together on the couch. I can only say that whenever Sandy and I are curled up so closely it only leads to one place. All in all, a perfect picture of a thoroughly contented family. We should all be so happy.

Lots of love, Honeypot.

Chapter Nineteen

There could never be any doubt about the guilt of Pat Hale, a.k.a. Pat Kerr. The presence of the stolen property in his employer's van along with his behaviour and the attempt to flee were more than sufficient. Fingerprint and handwriting evidence damned him in connection with the earlier cheque fraud on Henry Colebrook. He was also convicted of the armed robbery of Julian Blakelove QC.

Gemma Kendal, despite her plea of having acted under duress, was tried for complicity in the second of those two crimes. On her behalf, her QC pleaded that she had been led into mischief by her paramour and that her seduction of Mr Blakelove was the impetuous act of an infatuated woman with an excessive sex drive. She had agonised over whether to present to the court the picture of a dowdy countrywoman to whom sex would be a no-no or to portray a woman burdened with an unwanted beauty that attracted the attentions of men such as Mr

Blakelove. Vanity decided her to appear at her most seductive, which was a mistake. She might have escaped with a verdict of *not guilty*, or at the worst *not proven*, had her comment about Mr Blakelove's qualities as a lover not been leaked back to the QC himself. His description of the pleasure she had taken in tying him to the chair and taping his mouth was so detailed and graphic that a conviction was inevitable. She received a lesser sentence than did her lover.

The upper reaches of the legal profession had closed ranks in an attempt to spare Julian Blakelove embarrassment. The prosecution made no attempt to introduce in evidence the manner of Ms Kendal's dress (or undress) on the occasion of the robbery. It seemed, however, that her counsel was not acting wholly under pressure from those upper reaches – pressure that, as one who fervently disliked Mr Blakelove, he resented. Tipped off by a similarly motivated person (who shall be nameless but whose identity may well be guessed) he managed to leave the door open for Honey, in replying to a question about the accused's words on being arrested, to quote the remark about sex with Mr Blakelove resembling being raped by a sweaty and overweight warthog. The comment was widely quoted and never forgotten. Honey awaits, not without a little trepidation, the next occasion when he will have the opportunity to question her in court.

Vernon Colebrook accepted the greatest share in the blame for concealing the death of his father. He could hardly do otherwise – the evidence was overwhelming. Daniel, who had not impersonated his father and whose only known sin was silence, served a shorter sentence. It was evident (to the police if not to the court) that there had been another agreement, amounting to conspiracy, between the brothers with the intent of keeping at least one of them at liberty to manage the business and to provide the others with comfort and support. Leo Colebrook escaped conviction with a verdict of *not proven.* The firm survived but, in order to raise the tax and fines imposed, was forced to go public. Detective Inspector 'Honey' Laird came by a block of shares, a gift from her father.

Maggie McLaghan, née Hale, was convicted of the murder of Henry Colebrook, largely on the scientific evidence and the word of the three brothers. She denied the charge adamantly but made some damaging admissions in the heat of her trial. She will not be seen in public for several years yet.

Before these various crimes could come to trial, Detective Inspector Laird was delivered of a six-pound baby girl. Detective Super-intendent Blackhouse was accepted as godfather. Nobody could think of a convin-cing excuse for passing him by.

Andrew Gray has almost completely recovered from his wound. He and Jackie also are aiming for a baby. In the meantime, the dogs keep them fully occupied. Jackie (now Mrs Gray) even qualified, along with Spot, to enter a field trial. They were un-placed that time but received a certificate of merit.

The publishers hope that this book has given you enjoyable reading. Large Print Books are especially designed to be as easy to see and hold as possible. If you wish a complete list of our books please ask at your local library or write directly to:

Magna Large Print Books
Magna House, Long Preston,
Skipton, North Yorkshire.
BD23 4ND

This Large Print Book, for people
who cannot read normal print,
is published under the auspices of

THE ULVERSCROFT FOUNDATION

... we hope you have enjoyed this book.
Please think for a moment about those
who have worse eyesight than you ...
and are unable to even read or enjoy
Large Print without great difficulty.

You can help them by sending a
donation, large or small, to:

**The Ulverscroft Foundation,
1, The Green, Bradgate Road,
Anstey, Leicestershire, LE7 7FU,
England.**
or request a copy of our brochure for
more details.

The Foundation will use all donations
to assist those people who are visually
impaired and need special attention
with medical research, diagnosis
and treatment.

Thank you very much for your help.